Critical acclaim for the books in

Staffordshire Library and Information Services
Please return or renew by the last date shown

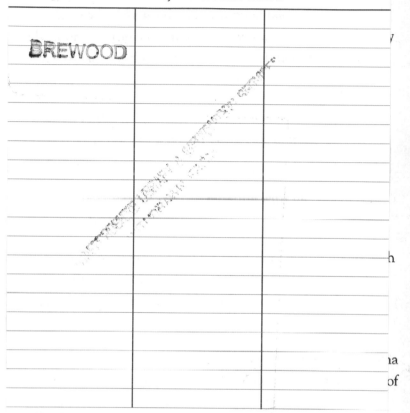

BREWOOD

It not required by other readers, this item may may be renewed in person, by post or telephone, online or by email. To renew, either the book or ticket are required

24 Hour Renewal Line
0845 33 00 740

Staffordshire
County Council

ending' *Times Edu*

STEPHEN POTTS

Stephen wanted to be a doctor from an early age. He studied hard, spending his spare time on the water, or with his head in a book. He has always read hungrily, from Cornflakes packets to Tolstoy, but didn't think about writing until medical school at Oxford. Initially he wrote as a distraction from exams, and subsequently as a relief from punishing hours as a junior doctor. The longer he's spent in medicine – he's now a consultant in an Edinburgh teaching hospital – the more seriously he's taken his writing. When he's not working on his next book, he's on his boat, together with his partner and a pair of young sea-dogs.

So far his books have been nominated for the Carnegie Medal (twice), the Branford-Boase Award, and the Askews prize, as well as translated into Japanese and optioned for feature films.

OTHER TITLES IN THE RUNNING TIDE SERIES

Compass Murphy
The Ship Thief

STEPHEN POTTS

HUNTING GUMNOR

EGMONT

To Letty and Terry, for all your love and support

EGMONT
We bring stories to life

First published 1999
by Mammoth, an imprint of Egmont Books Limited
Published in this edition 2004
239 Kensington High Street, London W8 6SA

ISBN 1 4052 0416 8

1 3 5 7 9 10 8 6 4 2

A CIP catalogue record for this title is available from the British Library

Typeset by Avon DataSet Ltd, Bidford on Avon, Warwickshire B50 4JH
Printed and bound in Great Britain by the CPI Group

'For most of my life I have messed about in boats, and at one point my home was a converted barge. I have lazed around in punts, paddled canoes, raced sculling boats and rowing eights, and sailed dinghies, yachts and tall ships on all kinds of water, from the Thames to the Caledonian Canal to the Arctic Ocean. I still get seasick.

This is a story about the sea, and sea people: but it can only be told through their boats, for they are inseparable. When you are next in a boat, listen to it. Let it tell you its stories. You might be surprised.'

Stephen

CONTENTS

CHAPTER ONE
THE VANISHING

MR BOOFUS STOPPED ROWING TO LISTEN. Water lapped at the bows of his boat, and fell in drops from his raised blades. A line of cormorants sped by, skimming the water with a whisk of wings. As they melted into the fog, and he listened harder, he could hear the engine choirs on the bridge high above, but he could hear nothing else.

He frowned and took up his oars again, moving with a crisp but easy rhythm, echoed in leathery creaks from his blades. As his breathing grew heavy, the clouds of moisture he exhaled hung in the air, depositing beads of dew on his fuzzy sideburns and the hairy backs of his hands. He knew the route so well, even in the fog, that when he first looked round for the landing stage, there it was before him, not twenty feet away. He drew close, shipped his oars, and tied up, then climbed stiffly out of the boat and up the steps.

He was very worried by the silence now, and when he reached the bridge's great tower, his bulky shoulders drooped as he saw what he'd feared most. A stout iron ring was set into the tower three feet from the ground. Running from it was a light chain which, on any other morning, would have reached the deep pool set into the concrete nearby. Today, instead, it ended abruptly, the final link broken cleanly across. The newly exposed metal shone brightly. Mr Boofus looked down, head bowed, at the way the broken chain had been neatly coiled. He stood statue-still, silent, then at length stooped forward, sighing, to pick up the pieces of the broken link. He pocketed them and paced around the platform, looking for some kind of clue. There were the usual scraps and fishy remnants – a backbone, a mackerel head picked clean by the gulls, a scattering of scales like wax drops from a candle – all leavings from a creature's meals, but of the creature herself there was no sign.

Mr Boofus stared out to sea, where the fog was beginning to thin as the October sun rose in the sky behind him. 'Oh, Gumnor,' he muttered solemnly. 'What will become of us now that you're gone?' And he clambered back into his boat with a heavy heart.

Rarty lay in bed watching her cat, Captain Peg, as he washed. He sat on the windowsill, framed by the early light pushing past the curtains. Voices drifted up from the kitchen below: her mother's, distraught and anxious, and her father's, soothing but sad. She slipped out of bed and down the stairs, the better to hear them.

Silence fell as she opened the door to the kitchen. Her mother turned to the pan of porridge bubbling on the hearth, while her father's comforting arm slipped back to his side.

''Tis early yet, Rarty,' said Mrs Boofus. 'Back to bed a while, lass.'

Rarty clung to the door handle. 'What is it, Ma? Something's wrong, isn't it?'

Mrs Boofus stirred the porridge abstractedly, but said nothing.

'Ma?'

Mrs Boofus set the ladle down and wiped her hands, turning to her husband. 'I'll set breakfast while you tell her, Lon.'

Mr Boofus took Rarty's hand and led her to the window. 'What do you see, Rarty?'

'Not a lot. There's still too much fog.'

'And what do you hear?'

'Nothing.'

'There you are then.'

'But I *don't* see. What do you mean, Pa?'

Rarty turned from the window to try and extract clues from her father's face. All she saw were the same weather-beaten cheeks, the same grey-blue eyes she knew and loved so well. Her frown grew deeper till realisation struck: 'Gumnor? Gone?' she cried, turning sharply back to the window as if she expected to see the great creature slipping away off to sea, a broken chain dangling loosely from her neck. 'Oh, Pa, no. No. Where? Why? How'd she break her chain?' She paused, but only for breath. 'Can we find her?'

'One at a time, lass, one at a time. I don't know where or why, except that she's been getting restless lately – you know that. I always thought she stayed because she wanted to, and not because my chains kept her there. Maybe she changed her mind.' He released her hand to straighten the sleep-tousled curls in her hair. 'As for finding, we'll look for her, won't we? No finding without looking.' She nodded. 'Get dressed now, child, and we'll start after breakfast.'

'You mean no school?' she asked, full of hope.

Mr Boofus hesitated. A few years ago there would have been no question of taking her off school, but now, old as he was, he needed her help. He smiled sadly at her, avoiding his wife's eyes. 'No school. Not today,' he said.

Rarty rushed off to dress, returning within minutes, apple-fresh and breathless, in a baggy jumper, patched and faded jeans, and scuffed tennis shoes. They sat down at the table while Mrs Boofus ladled out the thick grey porridge.

'Let's see you dress that fast on schooldays too then, shall we?' said Mr Boofus as he took up his spoon.

Breakfast ended with a loud knock at the door. Mrs Boofus stiffened. 'I fear that's Grundy, Lon. I didn't think he'd come so soon. What do we say?'

The knock came again, impatiently now. 'Let's find out what *he* has to say first, eh?' Mr Boofus went out to the hall, where he answered the door to an intense little man in a suit and tie, carrying an old brown briefcase. 'Morning, sir. You'll come in?'

'Good morning to you, Mr Boofus. I will, yes, thank you.'

Mr Boofus led him to the rarely used front room and offered him the best chair. Grundy sat down fussily, laid his briefcase across his knees and cleared his throat.

'Well, Mr Boofus. Um. What I've come about is . . . want to talk to you about . . . Well . . .'

'Gumnor, sir. I 'spect you've come about Gumnor.'

'Yes, that's right. What's happened? There was no fog warning this morning.'

'She's gone, sir.'

'Gone? But how? Where? I don't understand.'

'She's just not there no more, sir. She broke her chains in the night and she's gone, blowed if I know where.'

'I see. Mmm.' Grundy fiddled with his briefcase handles. 'This is very unfortunate, Mr Boofus. We must have a foghorn, you know that. I've already had a complaint from one skipper this morning. He came in with the tide overnight and nearly hit the northern tower.'

'I'm sorry, sir.' Mr Boofus stared at his boots. There had been no shipping accidents in his years at the bridge and, as a former seaman himself, he was very proud of his record.

Grundy felt awkward. 'I'm not blaming you, Boofus. I'm merely pointing out that we must have a foghorn. I have to decide what to do. Can you get the beast back or acquire another?'

Mr Boofus felt Grundy *was* blaming him. 'I can look for 'un, sir. Can't say as I'll be sure to find 'er. As for another, I fear she were one o' the last. I know not as there are many more. I think that's why she stayed – all her old haunts are empty now. Her kind may be gone.' He stared out of the window.

After a difficult pause Grundy sat up sharply. 'I have a suggestion.' He coughed. 'I'll give you a week to find the old beast or get a new one. We have a small electric horn we can use in the meantime.' Mr Boofus looked up as Grundy went on. 'If by next Tuesday you haven't been successful, I'm afraid I'll have to authorise a permanent replacement. With winter coming up we can't delay any longer than that. What do you say?'

Mr Boofus jumped up out of his seat and offered his hand. 'I'm very grateful, sir, thank you. Very grateful. I'll do everything I can. Thank you.'

Mr Boofus showed him out. Mrs Boofus stood in the hallway with her arms folded. She screwed up her courage to ask in a faltering voice, 'Mr Grundy? One question, Mr Grundy, sir.'

His hand fell back from the door knob, impatiently. 'Yes?'

'What happens if'n we don't find Gumnor and you get a 'lectric 'orn? I mean what happens to us? What about our cottage?' She gestured at the hallway in which they stood.

'That may be out of my hands, Mrs Boofus. I can't say. I don't know.' He looked embarrassed.

'Then we may have to leave?' she persisted, struggling to hide the tremble in her voice.

'I hope it won't come to that, but I honestly don't know. I'll do what I can to prevent it. And now I really must go. Good-day.' He slipped quickly out of the door and away, his trim little footsteps clipping down the path faster than usual.

To row the whole way across the strait when the tide was in full flood or ebb required strength and watermanship, and Rarty could see the effort and concentration on her father's face as he drew them along. The first bridge tower soon passed on the starboard side, but the second, the northern, approached very slowly. Mr Boofus was sweating, but he gruffly declined Rarty's offer of help. When at last they did reach the second tower, he tied up to rest for a while, gazing over her shoulder to the city shore, at something seen dimly through thinning fog.

'What is it, Pa?' but Rarty needed no answer, for she too could see the motor launch which had sped from the coastguard station on the shore, its white wake spreading wide behind it. They watched as it drew up to the southern tower – Gumnor's home – and moored there. Men in overalls lifted a bulky grey object out of the launch and on to the platform.

'What are they doing?' asked Rarty.

'It's the new horn, the 'lectric one.' Mr Boofus had seen enough. He clapped his hands and took up his oars once more. 'Cast off there, Rarty. Let's be making way.' The little boat moved off again, more purposefully now, and with less buffeting from the tide, as they neared the northern shore.

'All right now, children, settle down, settle down.' The hubbub slowly subsided. At the back of the room a paper aeroplane settled gently to the floor, disowned by its launcher.

Miss Fosby was not fooled. 'Pick it up, Lionel.' A child near the door made a poor attempt to look innocent, blushing at the giggles around him.

'It *is* yours, Lionel, isn't it?' He gave in and admitted ownership, then got up and sidled over to the plane, lying abandoned between desks. He retrieved it sheepishly and headed back to his seat.

'Here, Lionel. Bring it here. I don't want it flying again before break.' The giggles increased as Lionel walked his lonely way to the front to hand it over. As he returned, Miss Fosby noticed the empty desk: the only empty desk that day. 'Has anyone seen Rarty Boofus this morning?' Several small heads turned to the vacant place, as if they too were seeing it for the first time, and then back to Miss Fosby. None of them nodded. Miss Fosby felt a twinge of concern – Rarty was never late, and rarely ill – but she took care not to let it show. 'What do we do on Tuesday mornings, Lionel?' she asked, offering him a chance to redeem himself.

'Reading, Miss.'

'And what's the book we're reading now?'

'*Wind in the Willows*, Miss.'

'Would you like to read to us?' He smiled and nodded vigorously. All his blushes had gone.

'Pretty things, aren't they?' Mr Boofus asked as he paddled into the little marina beneath the bridge's northern end, weaving between the sleek yachts which bobbed brightly at anchor there.

'They're lovely, Pa,' Rarty replied, missing his mocking tone, and reaching for a rusty ladder set into the harbour wall. She scrambled out of the boat, made fast, and shouldered the haversack he passed her.

'City folks' boats these, lass, for weekending, that's all,' he grumbled, joining her on the jetty. They set off northwards along the shore, looking about for any sign of Gumnor. Rarty took the rocks by the water, her father the dunes behind. Three fruitless hours later, he called a break and returned to his theme. 'I wish I could show you a proper ship, lass. The bay was packed with them once.'

Rarty, who had heard this before, unwrapped their frugal lunch without replying. Instead she voiced the thoughts she had pondered all morning. 'Pa,' she enquired, handing him a sandwich, 'why should she just go like that? I mean, what more could she want? She had a lovely home under the bridge there, with free food, and ships to watch, and visits from us.'

Mr Boofus was silent for a while, staring seaward, before speaking in a softened tone. 'Rarty, all living creatures get old – hugumnodins no less than you or I or your wee cat. Eventually, when they get old enough, they die. Now, I don't know how old Gumnor was' – already he said 'was' not 'is' – 'but she'd been sat there by the bridge a good few years. I don't know how long hugumnodins live neither, but it ain't for ever. I fear the time had come for her to die, and she knew it. She wanted to return to her own for that, even though she were happy enough with us. P'raps she heard them calling.'

'But where do they all come from?' asked Rarty.

Mr Boofus shrugged. 'Who knows? They're creatures of the oceans, like fish or dolphins or whales, but their race is very old and now they number but a few. No one knows much about them, not even those professor chappies from the city. I had one round asking me questions some years back. He wanted to look over old Gumnor. Told me the proper name for them was *ceto- . . . cita- . . . cetylareans* or some such. Latin, he said it was. Meant they were like whales but different.'

'So why do we call them hugumnodins?'

'That's the name us sea people give them. From the old language.'

'What's it mean then?' asked Rarty, reaching for one of the two apples.

'It doesn't mean anything,' he replied, taking the other. 'It's a name, is all.' He held up his fruit and pointed out to sea. 'Now, you call this an apple. On the islands over there it's a "treppy".' He stood up and took a bite. 'Just names. An' now let's finish these treppies on the hoof.'

They swopped territories, Mr Boofus taking the shoreline and Rarty the dunes. As the sun touched the horizon Mr Boofus called out, 'Rarty?' She waved back. 'Enough for one day, eh?' She nodded agreement, and together they climbed the hill behind the shore. They paused for a breath-back rest on the summit, and saw below the sweeping curves of a busy road. The hurtling cars all had their lights on, but little of their noise reached the hilltop, where the wash of waves was still just audible. The sun was almost down, swallowed by a grey-pink sea, but the lingering glow it left in the west threw faint long-legged shadows before them as they strode on, over springy turf, to the bridge. Rarty pondered: a whole day gone, and no sign of Gumnor. There were only six days left.

Rarty retraced her steps with her father the following fogless dawn, yawning her way over the bridge to the northern harbour, where their battered boat looked out of place amid the snobby yachts. They paddled off to catch the tide as it streamed out through the gate, and used it to carry the boat well up the coast, beyond where they'd finished the day before. The shoreline looked very different from the seaward side. 'We didn't come this far did we, Pa?' Rarty had never seen this stretch of coast before.

'No, love, we did not.' Mr Boofus appeared tense and worried now. He looked round frequently.

Rarty followed his stares. At first she saw nothing, although she could hear a distant buzzing noise, like an angry wasp. The noise grew louder and then she spotted, off the port beam, a distant grey object which hurtled towards them, trailing a huge wake. She jumped up. 'Pa!' she exclaimed, pointing over his shoulder. 'Pa, look!'

He stopped rowing, and grunted when he saw it too. 'Humph! I thought as much.'

'What is it, Pa? What is it?'

It was a motor patrol boat, riding high in the water in a roar of spray and engines, and bearing a number – SVB-25-11 – where other craft carry names. Its surging wash broke over the rowing boat's gunwale, shocking Rarty with a cold salty splash. She clung tightly to her seat as the boat dipped and rolled, and water sloshed round her feet. The patrol boat slowed and circled round ahead to approach from the starboard, shoreward side. It drew up slowly, like a watchful sheepdog herding a stray. The thunder of its engines died to a dull throbbing, barely heard above the splashing of the last of the wash. As this faded there was an ominous quiet.

A small man in a dark uniform peered at them from the deck of the vessel, and another taller one, from the cabin near the stern. He wore an officer's cap, and held a microphone.

Rarty was frightened. 'Pa?' she asked in a quavery voice. He looked back at her and said something, but his words were lost as a harsh metallic voice thundered out from loudspeakers on the patrol boat's bows.

'HEAVE TO. HEAVE TO AND BE INSPECTED. THIS IS A FORBIDDEN AREA.'

The officer snapped out instructions to Mr Boofus and his own crew, and the two craft drew together until they rubbed alongside. The patrol boat's shadow closed over them like a cloak. The other man came to the railings and peered down with a cold hard stare. Without a word he dropped a rope for Mr Boofus to make fast. When Rarty next looked up, the sailor had been joined by the officer, who demanded to know who they were and what they were doing there.

Mr Boofus explained apologetically. 'Beg pardon, sir, I'm the keeper of the bridge foghorn, and this here's my daughter.' It pained Rarty to see her father so submissive, especially since the wash had soaked him too. Anger soon replaced her fear, as he continued, 'We're searching for our beast, who has gone from her lair on the bridge since yesterday. We mean no harm, sir. I had no knowledge this area was the Navy's.'

The officer leaned closer. 'Well, foghorn keeper, the Navy's it is. You may not pass within four miles of that tower you see there.' He pointed to a radio mast on the cliffs. 'And you are closer to three. I shall escort you ashore and out of this zone, and warn you that to be found here again will mean your arrest. Good-day to you.'

Rarty glared up at the officer. She held his gaze while she pointedly baled out below him, flinging water at the patrol boat's indifferent hull. He watched her a while. 'Shouldn't your child be at school, Boofus?' he asked frostily, then stepped briskly back into the cabin.

The patrol boat towed them slowly on a long line. Fifty yards from shore it stopped so Mr Boofus could cast off. The cold-eyed sailor coiled up the line and signalled to the cabin. Without a word or a wave they accelerated hard and swept away seawards.

Rarty and her father watched them go in silence, until their boat grounded on the shingle beach. Rarty took the painter and leapt from the bows, timing her jump to avoid the waves. When the next large wave came, she backed up the beach, pulling hard to draw the boat up. As the wave receded, Mr Boofus clambered out. He stretched the rowing stiffness out of his joints, while Rarty scouted round for a long stick. She drove it down into the pebbles until it stood upright, and then piled several large stones round its base to hold it firmly in place. This done, she tied the boat's painter to it.

'Round turn and two half-hitches, Rarty.'

Rarty was relieved by this end to the awkward silence. 'I know.'

'Then why did you tie a granny, eh?' He made her check. She retied it without comment, then they set off southwards, clattering over the pebbles.

Questions bubbled up within her. 'Why'd you let them be so nasty to us, Pa?'

'It doesn't do to get tangled up with these people, lass. I saw you a-steamin' up with the officer back there. There'd be nothing but trouble if you'd spoken out. You don't know what they're like.' He tossed a pebble into the surf. 'I've 'eard stories of folk 'ereabouts goin' off fishin', never to be seen again, just their boats found driftin' empty.' Rarty shuddered. 'I didn't mean to go as close as I did, and last time I fetched up here I was told it was three miles, anyway.'

As they moved on, the sky began to cloud over, and the sun disappeared from time to time, bringing a chill to the air. They spent the morning scouring the beach and the grasslands that led down to it. Just before noon they came upon a tiny white-washed cottage, huddled at the base of a low hill. The windows were shuttered, there was a double front door, and a grass-covered bank rose in front, all for protection from the storms which would surely follow later in the winter. At present the shutters were open, and a light curl of peat smoke rose from the single chimney. There were nets and lobster pots strewn by the open front door, and a rusting anchor stood propped against the wall.

'Hello?' called Mr Boofus. 'Hello, John? Anyone

home?' There was no reply to this or to his loud knocking on the door. Mr Boofus shrugged and walked away. 'Maybe we'll catch him on the way back.'

'Who, Pa?' asked Rarty, reluctantly following. 'Who is it lives there?'

'A friend of mine from years back. We sailed together. On the *Unicorn*. Haven't seen him for a long time now.' He fell silent, looking out to sea with a faraway stare.

Before long the pebble beach gave way to the rocky jumble familiar from the previous day. After an hour or so of scrambling, Mr Boofus stopped, looked up towards the sun and then down at the shore. 'See that, Rarty?' he asked, pointing at the water's edge. 'Tide's turning. And so are we. This is where we got to yes'day. Back to the boat, now, lass. There's nothing for us this side of the gate.'

Returning to the pebble beach, Rarty spotted a white-haired figure bent under the weight of a clutch of lobster pots. Behind him on the shingle lay a boat just like their own.

'Ho there! Ho there, John Quarrie!' Mr Boofus called, waving vigorously. 'Let's give him a hand with those pots, lass,' he said to Rarty, as he quickened the scrunch of his steps.

The fisherman stopped and stared. His eyes flitted

uncertainly from one face to the other as they approached. A smile suddenly cracked his heavily weathered face. He dropped his gear and held out his hand. 'Lon Boofus! Well I never!' His voice rasped as if it was little used, and he wheezed when he breathed.

'It's been years, Lon. How are you?' They shook hands warmly. 'This 'ere must be your lass,' he said, patting Rarty on the head. 'Fine young girl.' He bent low to pat her cheek.

Rarty shrank back from the fishy fumes he breathed. She pointed at the lobster pots. 'Can I help?' she asked.

'Why, that's kind,' said John Quarrie. 'You take this one.' It was empty, like the others. A few scrawny crabs wriggled in his bucket, but that was the extent of his haul.

Mr Boofus eyed the bucket. 'Catches down, eh, John?' he asked.

'Aye. It's grim. You can see for yourself there's no lobsters any more, and the fish get smaller all the time. I barely make a living. I put it all down to the Navy folk. Coming and going at all hours, day and night, lights flashing, funny noises. I'd move right away if I'd somewhere to go, but I ain't.' He switched the bucket to his other hand. 'Anyways, you still ain't said what brings you 'ere. Nobody comes all this way just to visit.'

Mr Boofus explained about Gumnor. John Quarrie shook his head. 'A shame, so it is, Lon. I'll certainly look out for any sign of 'er.' He stopped and set down his load. They'd reached his cottage. 'But you're not the first to come searchin' round 'ere, lately. Night before last I had a lot of they Navy fellows trampin' over the beach 'ere, and a-bangin' on the door at night. Asked me if I'd seen anythin' funny or different, but I couldn't say as I 'ad. They wanted me to keep my eyes open too.'

Rarty's curiosity was aroused. 'What were they looking for?'

'Blowed if I know, lassie. They wouldn't tell me – but I over'eard some of them talkin'. Submarines close to shore, or some such. They searched land and sea for hours. Didn't find nothin', though.' He stacked the empty lobster pots. 'You'll come in?' he asked hesitantly.

'Thank you, John, but no,' Mr Boofus declined before Rarty could speak. 'We've the tide to catch. We'll be searching south of the gate tomorrow.'

John Quarrie nodded and held out his hand. 'It's been good to see you, Lon. Not so long, next time, eh?'

'Bye, Mr Quarrie,' said Rarty. She wanted to ask him more, but her father led her away. When she looked back to wave, he was stooped in front of his cottage, fiddling with his nets. He straightened and waved back stiffly.

* * *

'Single please, Mrs B.' Mrs Boofus looked up at the customer offering her coins through the kiosk window. It was Mrs Flaggins, an islander, taking the ferry home. 'Sorry to hear about your trouble,' she said. 'We're all looking around on the islands, but no news yet, I'm afraid.'

Mrs Boofus handed her a ticket. 'Thank you, Jinty. It's kind of you. I don't know what we shall do if we can't find her. Lon's out searching high and low, and Rarty's off school to help. I don't like it, but we've little choice.'

Mrs Flaggins pocketed the change. 'I know. There's no future without schooling for our youngsters these days, but when they do get it they don't want to stay on the islands. Take Jack Copley's young lad – what's his name?'

'Luke, isn't it?'

'Luke, then. Anyway, young Luke's leaving for the city in the spring. Not two years out of school and already he's decided that island life is not for him. His pa's proper upset, he is. Mind you, we can't blame the young folk really, can we? There's not much on the islands for them any more, and it's harder than ever to make a living from the fish.'

'That's right,' said Mrs Boofus wearily. Once Mrs Flaggins started chatting it was hard to stop her, and the

21

ferry was not due for a while. Mrs Boofus was resigned to an onslaught of chitchat, when someone else strode briskly up to her kiosk. Recognising him as a city type, Mrs Flaggins fell silent and stepped aside, taking care to remain within earshot. Only a stern stare from the man, through frameless glasses which magnified his eyes, made her back away. He turned back to the window. 'Where to, sir?' asked Mrs Boofus uncertainly.

'I'm not going anywhere,' he replied tetchily. 'I'm looking for someone. A Mrs Boofus. I believe she works here.'

'I'm she. How can I help?'

The man glanced at Mrs Flaggins, already edging closer again. 'Can we talk in private?' he asked.

'Of course,' said Mrs Boofus. She let him in and sat him down.

He coughed and introduced himself. 'My name is George Ellard. I'm the city school attendance officer. I'm here about your daughter.'

'I see,' said Mrs Boofus anxiously. She was shocked that he'd come so soon.

'She's not at school today. Nor was she there yesterday. I hope she's not unwell. You see, Mr Grundy told her teacher about the misfortune with the . . . the, ah, beast. He knew how fond your daughter was of it, and worried she might be too upset for school. Kind of him, I thought. Well, when Rarty didn't come to school again, naturally I was informed and –'

'She's helping her father,' broke in Mrs Boofus. 'They're out looking for the beast, as you call her, right now.'

'That may be so, Mrs Boofus. But we cannot allow children to be taken out of school at the whim of their parents. It disrupts their education.'

''Tis no whim, Mr Ellard. We have no wish to take her from school, especially now that she is starting to do well.'

Ellard softened a little. 'Yes, I believe she's top of her class. And normally her attendance is exemplary.'

'I know it. I make sure of it.' Her voice was rising. 'Only now our livelihood depends upon finding Gumnor – the beast, that is – and her help is needed.'

'I'm sorry to hear that. But our rules cannot allow this sort of absence. The only reason that will do is if she's ill and has a doctor's note. May we see her in class tomorrow?' He stood up, clearly wishing to end the conversation. Mrs Boofus sat still, looking at his chair and picking at the buttons on her dress. 'Oh dear! Oh dear, oh dear.'

Mr Ellard turned back and bent awkwardly to touch her on the arm. 'Mrs Boofus,' he said. She ignored him at first. 'Mrs Boofus . . . I think you have a customer.' She gave a little start, looked round at the kiosk counter, where a queue of ferry passengers was forming, and stood up sharply.

'Yes, Mr Ellard, she'll go tomorrow. I'm sorry for your trouble.' She gathered herself together and showed him out, then settled down at her counter to issue tickets again.

'Why didn't we go in, Pa?' asked Rarty. They were back at their boat.

Mr Boofus kicked away the boulders she had piled round the mooring stick. 'He's a poor man, Rarty. He keeps his house open because there is nothing there to steal. I looked inside.' He gave the stick a tug and it popped free. 'It's a dreadful clutter, and there'd be little enough food in the larder for one. He'd have felt bad letting us see him and his place like that, and he'd have starved rather than not give us some vittles, for he's proud. I didn't want him to do that. It's a shame.'

While he fiddled with Rarty's knot, she ran her eyes over the forbidden cliffs. There were marines, two or three at first, in grey-green uniforms, moving along the top. More emerged from a dell, where the cliffs had slipped. They gestured to the others and pointed at the dell, into which they all then vanished. Rarty said nothing.

They dragged the boat to the water's edge. Mr Boofus hauled himself in between waves, then Rarty pushed the boat afloat and jumped in after him. She sat looking over her father's shoulder to the shore, while he paddled away on the gathering tide. A jeep-load of marines arrived at the dell as she watched.

'Your eyes look fit to pop, lass. What is it?'

'N-nothing, Pa.' She'd never lied before. 'I thought I saw a seal.' She didn't understand what stopped her telling him the truth, and fell into a troubled frowning silence.

Her father paddled on. 'Penny for your thoughts, my girl.' Rarty stumbled for words. She couldn't tell him what was really on her mind – that she *knew* he was wrong to head south – so, to cover up, she asked a question she'd often pondered on foggy nights a-bed and always forgot the next day.

'Pa? Why *does* Gumnor make that noise in the fog? What is she saying?'

'It's one of their natural 'abits. They call so in the wild, no less than when they're tamed. Many's the tale about the whys and wherefores, especially among us old sailors.' Rarty relaxed to listen to him talk, as the tide swept them back to the gate. 'I'm not sure as anyone knows the truth. Some say they do it to lure ships rockwards, but I reckon that's superstitious malarkey. We 'eard 'em on the clippers, and never were endangered.

'There's others would tell you they call to proclaim their domain, like robins in spring. I asked that professor fellow what he thought. He said it's their courtship. When they're ready to bear young, other creatures meet up, one with another, in pairs – but not hugumnodins. No, they gather first, in a great meeting, as many of 'em as are in range. He reckoned it could be hundreds when they were common, enough to make the sea boil. Seems that when they are all together, they're easy prey for sharks and suchlike, so they meet briefly and only ever in the fog, before they scatter in pairs. Their fogblast noise is a call to a meeting.'

He paused, to wipe the sweat from his brow. His tone was different when he spoke once more. 'These meetings don't happen now, least not for us to see, as there's so few left, but still, when the fog comes, they make the call. It's like ringing a church bell to bring folk to service, only no one ever turns up.'

Rarty knew well the yearning in Gumnor's voice which carried with her call along the coasts and over the rooftops of the sleeping city. Islanders, city folk, passing sailors – all would stop to listen, and to feel the pangs of sadness the sounds brought. Even the citysiders knew the difference between Gumnor's eerie cries and the flat, lifeless tone of the mechanical foghorns on the ships that passed her by.

Now she understood. Gumnor's call was a huge roar of loneliness, of longing for the company of other *Cetylareans*, for the great gatherings they once knew, after one of which Gumnor herself had begun. It was an aching lament for the passing of her kind and the world they had inhabited.

CHAPTER TWO
KRAKEN

'TIS FOR THE BEST, RARTY,' SAID MRS BOOFUS, as the bus bumbled along the windswept waterfront. 'And it's not just your pa and me saying so. That Mr Ellard, he wants you in school, too. Even if we kept you away, he'd make you go. It's the law.'

'Well, the law's wrong. Poor old Pa, trudging off on his own like that, and me kept from helping.' That morning, in the storm's first grumblings, she had watched her father don his oilskins and splash off towards the southern cliffs. Wild though the weather was, she'd dearly wished to go there with him, not polish her new shoes for school in the city.

'I didn't want him to go neither,' said Mrs Boofus. 'And if I didn't have to work to support us now, I'd be there with him. But you remember, Rarty, when we talked about it last night, he wanted you back at school as well. We're all agreed that it's best.'

I'm *not* agreed, thought Rarty, but she said nothing and lapsed into a moody stare out of the window. They were passing the last of the docks, whose great cranes stood like herons, swinging boxes from their beaks.

The bus came to a halt. 'Here's your stop,' said Mrs Boofus. 'You mind you cheer up, lass, or I'll not take you down to the *Kraken* after all.' She had promised Rarty a lunch-time trip to sweeten her return to class.

Rarty sat through the first lesson, geography, trying to concentrate, but her attention kept drifting away to the coasts where her father now clambered. For maths, which followed, she didn't even try. Instead she watched the raindrops as they ran down the window to merge in a puddle below. Outside, the sodden playing fields lay deserted. Rarty watched a group of wind-tugged seagulls fly away, silhouetted against the dark clouds growling over the horizon. It was a horrible day.

The teacher – nicknamed Ringo, though no one knew why – soon lost his patience. His chalk flew across the room and crashed against the wall above Rarty's head, showering her with fragments. She gave a violent start, and looked round, wide-eyed. The other children stifled sniggers. Ringo had a reputation for hurling objects at inattentive pupils, combined, by good fortune, with poor eyesight and consequently low accuracy. The children loved to see him angry, so long as they were not his target.

'Miss Boofus,' he roared, 'what answer do you have for question three?' Rarty had none, and everyone knew it. She scanned her textbook to see if she could guess something that sounded right, but the problem's complexity defeated her and she explained, in a thin, hesitant voice, that she had no answer at all. Ringo was in his element now. 'Very well. Question two, perhaps?' Again Rarty could offer nothing. Ringo drew closer, and stopped by her desk. 'Question one, then. Give us all the answer to question one. Stand up and shout it out.'

Rarty stood up, trembling. 'I don't know, sir,' she said almost inaudibly and close to tears.

'We can't hear you,' said Ringo, and goaded her into repeating her admission more loudly. 'Show me your work for this lesson,' he said, picking up her exercise book. Its pages were blank. He displayed it to the class, provoking their giggles.

After a long, melodramatic pause, he slammed the book down on her desk, and said angrily, 'Young lady, this is a maths lesson, not a nature ramble. You will stop staring out of the window when you should be working, and to make that easier for you, you will change places with . . . with . . . with Merry there.' He pointed to Lionel in the far corner. 'And to make sure you pay more attention in future, you will come and see me after school tomorrow to make up for the time you have lost today. Do you understand?'

Rarty gathered her books and moved across the room as instructed. She passed Lionel Merry halfway. He was not cruel like some of the others, and he gave her a little smile to try and help her feel better. All it did was bring her tears to the surface, but it was not until Ringo had resumed the lesson, and the children's attention had moved back to the blackboard, that she allowed herself to reach for her handkerchief to dry her eyes.

At morning break Rarty avoided the other children, though this was difficult, as the weather kept them indoors. Her class always spent rainy breaktimes in the biology room, surrounded by stuffed birds and pickled fish. While the others chattered loudly, and the prefect struggled to keep order, Rarty wandered round the room, gazing at the specimens.

On a dusty corner shelf, between a startled pine marten and a mournful, moth-eaten owl, she came across a pile of old books she had not seen before. She picked up the topmost, entitled *Creatures of the Sea* and looked up 'hugumnodin' in the index. There was no entry under that name, nor under *Cetylarean*. She tried the next, a heavy, musty-smelling volume, with dog-eared corners and a scratched leather cover. It had a page about *Cetylareans*, with a picture, though this was a drawing, not a photograph, and looked nothing like Gumnor. She read on anyway:

> . . . *these unusual creatures sometimes attain a length of thirty feet or more, and a weight of many tons. They feed almost exclusively on fish, in contrast to the whale, with which they are often confused, and to which they are, albeit distantly, related. A further contrast lies in the means of reproduction, the* Cetylarean *being oviparous, while whales, like other mammals, exhibit viviparity.*

The book went on, but told her nothing new or used big words she didn't understand. The break-end bell found her tracing one of them – 'oviparous' – on to the back of her hand.

Rarty swung gently in the canvas hammock, listening to the *Kraken*'s chorus of ship sounds. Rain pattered steadily on the deck above, accompanied by timber-creaks and the rustle of the hammock cloth. Wind whistled through the rigging high aloft, cracking the flags and clapping ropes against the masts. She closed her eyes and added, in her imagination, sharp orders from the deck officer to the helmsman, and the chatter of off-watch sailors in the fo'c'sle around her.

Rarty loved to visit the *Kraken*, an old three-master, now carefully restored and preserved in the docks as a museum ship. It was best when, as now, there was no one else about, and she could sneak into the forbidden hammocks to daydream. She pictured Scots Tom, a homesick sailor berthed nearby, and hummed along with his melancholy mouth-organ lament, till eight bells sounded, when she slipped out of the hammock to go on watch above.

Huddled against the wind and rain, she went astern to the helm. She had to stretch to reach the handles on either side of the enormous wheel. She could barely see over the edge of the tall brass compass before her, and certainly couldn't say what the current heading was. The weather dampened her taste for fantasy here, so she dropped down the companionway nearby into the officers' quarters. The captain's cabin retained its original furnishings, so luxurious after the spartan utility of the crew deck.

Visitors were excluded by a thick red rope slung waist-high across the cabin door, but they could gaze freely at all the accessories of the maritime life. There was a chart table with yellowing maps, a heavy logbook, and some old brass navigation instruments laid out on top. A pair of deep leather armchairs flanked the table, facing away to look out, as Rarty now did, through the magnificent stern window. All she could see was the grimy quayside, its hard edges softened by the still-heavy rain, but when she ducked under the rope and curled up in the starboard chair, it was easy to picture an empty seascape, and the ship's white wake trailing away to the horizon where a golden sun settled slowly down.

Her mother's voice from above snapped her back to reality. 'Rarty? Where are you? Rarty? Time to go, dear.'

The cottage was like a laundry-room. Steam rose from the pan of potatoes on the stove, and condensed on the windows to blot out the cloud-tumbled twilight sky. Another indoor cloud billowed upwards from the bathtub in front of the fire where Rarty was washing her hair, eyes shut tight against the soap. 'Ready, Ma,' she called.

Mrs Boofus set to with the rinsing jug. 'Shepherd's pie tonight,' she said. 'And your pa will need it.'

'I hope there's a lot,' said Rarty, beaming broadly. Meat was a special-occasion rarity in their cottage. ''Cos I'm starving.'

Mrs Boofus smiled. 'Never fear. There'll be enough for all and more.' She stood up. 'There. You're done. Mind you don't drip all over the floor when you get out.'

Rarty lay back in the tub to watch the fire. A curious Captain Peg appeared on the chair beside her and reached out tentatively with one paw for the puzzling mass of bubbles. Rarty roused herself. 'Come on, skipper,' she said. 'We can't stay here for ever.' She stood up, wrapped herself in the warm heavy folds of her towel, and disappeared to her bedroom to change.

'More logs there, Rarty, would you?' asked Mrs Boofus from the stove, when Rarty returned. Before she could reply there was a loud splash. Captain Peg had fallen into the tub, and was now frantically struggling to get out. He mewed furiously, scrabbling on the metal with his claws.

'You silly thing,' laughed Rarty, as she hauled him out. Mrs Boofus handed Rarty an old tea-towel to dry him off. They were still giggling at how small and oddly lumpy he looked, in his water-matted fur and soap-sud wig, when the door opened and Mr Boofus squelched into the kitchen.

Their laughter stopped dead when they saw him,

motionless in the doorway. His cheeks were whipped red by the wind, his lips were chapped and swollen, and blue hands dangled limply from his sleeves. Water streamed off his oilskins, over his muddy boots, and on to the floor. Rivulets of rain trickled down his face, from the sodden locks of hair emerging beneath his hat. One drop hung, quivering, from the end of his nose. He managed a smile, with an obvious effort, and a quiet greeting, which broke Mrs Boofus free of her immobility.

'Lon,' she cried, rushing over to him, 'look at you! You must be icy cold.'

'I am that,' he admitted, as he tried to undo the buttons of his jacket. His hands, numb with cold, were unequal to the task, and he submitted readily when his wife took over. Rarty shut the door behind him and piled all the remaining logs on the fire. Once free of his boots and oilskins, Mr Boofus closed up to the fire, his half-dead hands stretched out before him. He grinned, but did not laugh, when he learnt of Captain Peg's ducking. 'I told you he was stupid,' he said quietly, between shivers.

Rarty watched the steam rise from his clothes, sodden despite the oilskins. 'No luck, Pa?' she asked.

Mr Boofus shook his head. 'Not a trace. Nothing.' He turned to warm his back. 'I've been all the way down to Parrot Rock and back, and seen no sign at all.' His voice was flat and he didn't look up. Rarty had never seen him this way before. 'I'm beginning to think we shall never find her, Rarty, though not for want of trying.' He fell silent, turning back to stare into the fire. Mrs Boofus bustled Rarty off to fetch him some clean clothes.

After dinner Rarty retired with Captain Peg to her room to do her homework. She tried to concentrate, but soon found herself staring at the back of her hand and noticed that the writing had almost washed off in the bath. She picked up her pen and absentmindedly traced over the letters again, O-V-I-P-A-R-O-U-S, humming to herself the while.

When she looked into the kitchen to say goodnight, she found her parents sitting quietly in front of the fire. They didn't hear her enter.

'But if the weather's bad again, I'll take the bus to Tarnmouth and walk back to Parrot Rock,' said Mr Boofus. 'Two days' soaking would be too much.'

'What about the islands? Is it worth searching there? There's people looking about for us, but p'raps we could go there come the weekend and see for ourselves. Rarty and me could come with you.'

'Yes, yes we could.' Rarty's sudden plea startled them. 'Please, Pa,' she entreated.

'Let me think on that, lass,' he said. 'If I've no luck

tomorrow I daresay there's little else to try.' He held out his arms with a smile. 'But right now it's bedtime, my girl.'

'OK, Pa. G'night.' She kissed him, and turned to her mother. 'I might be a tad late home tomorrow, Ma.' She couldn't meet her mother's eye. 'There's something I have to stay behind for.'

Mrs Boofus quickly picked up her hesitant tone. 'Oh, what's that? Not in trouble, are you?'

Rarty blustered. 'No, no trouble, no. I've got to . . . I've got to catch up on what I missed, that's all. G'night.' She left before any more questions came her way.

The night before, tired by all her beachy tramping, she'd found sleep within minutes. Tonight, the image of her father dripping in the kitchen kept returning to trouble her, and she couldn't forget his quiet dejection over dinner. On top of it all, he was persisting in his plans to search southwards. She *knew* his hunt there would be futile, and she hated to think of him coming home again, even more downhearted. Rarty was convinced that if Gumnor was to be found anywhere it would be to the north, in the dell where she'd seen the marines the day before. And all she had to look forward to was another day at school, and a detention from Ringo to cap it off.

These thoughts ran round and round in her mind,

holding sleep at bay with an endless game of tag. The noises of the storm only increased her restlessness. The trees swished and creaked, and there were bangs and scrapings in the yard. Captain Peg sat on the windowsill, starting at each new crash. Rarty got up to join him. She knelt on the floor, placed her elbows on the windowsill, and laid her head in her cupped hands. 'What shall we do, skipper?' she sighed. 'Whatever shall we do?'

She shivered a while amid the window-rattling gusts until an idea suddenly burst through. She stood up briskly.

'Captain Peg,' she declared. '*I'm* going to find Gumnor. Tomorrow.'

She stood for a while, putting together a plan in her head, then dug a battered haversack out of her cupboard and filled it with old clothes. She nudged Captain Peg on to the floor and opened the window.

The chilly wind swirled round her, but she couldn't tell if it was the cold or her nerves which raised the goose-pimples on her arms. She hesitated a moment, staring out into the blustery night, then swallowed hard and stepped gingerly on to the sloping roof below. The cold patter of rain on her shoulders made her shiver, and the fear in her guts made her shake, but there was no turning back now.

Her dressing-gown flapped like a go-about sail as she

slithered down and made her way to the tool-shed. The door was unlocked but had stuck fast with the wet, and at first it would not budge. She put the haversack down and gave an almighty tug with both hands. The door flew open, and she staggered backwards, arms flailing. A nearby bush saved her from a full-length sprawl in the mud but, even so, she emerged soaked, scratched and dishevelled.

She hid the haversack under a tarpaulin at the back of the shed, closed the door, and hurried back to her window, where a curious Captain Peg greeted her as she clambered back inside and listened intently. She was sure her parents must have heard something. But the same low murmuring, with longer spells of silence, came through the floor, just as before. She was safe.

She jumped into her still-warm bed. As her shivering stopped she felt, at last, the beginnings of sleep sneak up on her. Through the gap where her curtains didn't meet she could see, beyond the ridge of the hill, the aircraft warning lights at the very top of the bridge's two towers. They blinked on and off, redly, through the rain, with a slow steady rhythm. Sometimes she would watch the lights and count their flashes. She had never got beyond two hundred. Tonight, tired as she now was, she was already half asleep when she reached twenty-five. The last thing she remembered was a gentle pressure on her legs as Captain Peg leapt on to the foot of the bed at thirty-seven.

CHAPTER THREE
TRUANT

THERE WAS A FRESHNESS IN THE AIR THE next morning, now that the storm had passed. The ground was sodden, with puddles everywhere, and drips still fell from the trees; but the windless sky was bright, and the birds sang loudly, glad for the abundance of worms washed to the surface of the soil.

Rarty waved her mother a cheery goodbye as she stepped down from the bus, and headed towards the school gates. She tried to behave as on any other schoolday, but her heart was hammering and her mouth was so dry her lips stuck to her teeth when she smiled her farewell. She walked slowly, to make sure the bus would be gone before she reached the gates, but Charlie, the driver, was in no hurry to leave. Her mother's eyes were upon her still and now, with the gates just yards away, she felt a rising sense of panic. If she didn't go in, her mother would see, but if she did, the teachers wouldn't let her leave again. She had to think of something fast.

She stopped abruptly, just short of the gates, and bent as if to tie her shoelaces, turning to watch the bus from the corner of her eye as she did so. At last Charlie stopped nattering, engaged gear and pulled away. The instant the bus disappeared round the corner, Rarty dashed for the cover of some trees nearby where she hid, trembling, desperately hoping she hadn't been spotted. No one shouted or followed her, and soon the school bell sounded. The noise in the playground reached a climax, then died away, as the children filed into their classrooms.

Rarty waited for Lionel Merry, who she knew would be late, because he always was. She heard him before she saw him, as he trotted up, talking to himself in the voice of Mr Ridley, the geography teacher.

'Late again, Lionel? Any new excuses, or just the same old ones rehashed?' Rarty couldn't help laughing. Lionel was a playground comic. His high-voiced Mr Ridley impression was especially good. There were times when his performances had the other children giggling uncontrollably, teary-cyed, but these usually ended with a stern-faced teacher awarding him yet another detention. Lionel was scruffy and disorganised, had few close friends, and didn't seem to care what the teachers thought of him. Rarty liked him, though he didn't know it.

Rarty peeped out from behind the tree to watch as he approached, shirt tails flapping. He stopped abruptly, threw back his head to look down his long nose, and snorted a perfect Miss Cranley snort. The voice, when it came, was as incongruously deep as Mr Ridley's had been high.

'Lionel Merry. Humph. Lionel Merry, you really are an awful, awful, *awful* little boy. Look at you.' He tucked in his shirt, straightened his tie, and pulled up his socks. 'And look at the time.' He looked at his watch. 'After cleanliness, punctuality is next to godliness, and you, young man, show no inclination to either. I fear for your soul. Get into class at once, boy.'

Rarty couldn't help laughing out loud. She stifled it halfway through and whipped back behind the tree, but it was too late. He had seen her. Lionel slipped out of his Miss Cranley role for the briefest of moments, just long enough to look round for any teachers nearby. He clasped his hands together and imitated Miss Cranley's stiff-kneed walk in waddling over to Rarty's tree.

44

'A surprise, Miss Boofus, I have to say a surprise. I am confident you have an explanation. Pray offer it.'

Rarty couldn't speak.

'No explanation? I am disappointed. Accompany me to your class and see me at break. Perhaps by then you will have a reason for your behaviour.'

Rarty was now laughing uncontrollably. 'Stop it. Stop it. Please stop.'

A smile twisted across Lionel's mouth, but he persisted with Miss Cranley. 'Stop *what* precisely? Please identify that which you would have me cease.' At last his composure was beginning to falter. 'I cannot cease what you will not . . .' and he too collapsed in peals of laughter.

They both hid behind the tree, red-faced, struggling to keep quiet, with hands over their mouths. They had to avoid each other's gaze, for each time their eyes met one of them would start laughing again and the other would join in. Eventually the silences between laughing spasms grew longer. During these, Rarty noticed her sides were hurting. She didn't know whether it was from laughing or from trying to stop.

Eventually Lionel found enough control to speak. 'What are you doing? Where are you sneaking off to?'

'I can't say.'

'You mean you *won't* say.'

'I can't tell you.'

'Why not? What's the secret?' Lionel knew Rarty had never bunked off school before. There had to be a special reason. 'I won't tell anyone,' he said.

'I'm sorry, Lionel. I just can't tell you. Please don't ask any more.' She no longer felt like laughing.

'Is it to do with your gumnor?' Rarty said nothing, but her silence and her eyes told him he was right. 'It *is* the gumnor, isn't it? You're missing school to look for it, aren't you?'

Rarty nodded and looked away. She never could keep secrets.

'Can I come?' he asked quietly.

Rarty looked up sharply. 'No. No you can't. I have to do this on my own.'

'Why on your own? Aren't you going with your dad?'

Rarty shook her head. 'He says I have to go to school. And anyway he's looking in the wrong place.'

'How do you know?'

'I just do. Now stop asking me all these questions. I'm going.'

'If you don't let me come with you I'll go and get a teacher.' He paused, and she looked at him. They both knew he wouldn't. He had to try something else. 'Or

46

I'll follow you. You can't stop me doing that.'

Rarty saw that she had little choice, but still tried to put him off. 'You're not dressed for it, or anything. You need old clothes for where I'm going. I've got some to change into. People will see your uniform and know you're skipping school.'

Lionel looked up. 'The weather's all right – we won't get soaked today.' He looked down. 'My shoes are good. I climb about in them all the time.' He took off his jacket and strapped it, rolled lengthways, to his satchel. 'And now I don't look like I'm missing school at all.'

Rarty conceded defeat. 'Oh, all right. But I'll leave you behind if you slow me down, and you must be quiet when I tell you, and you must do what I say.'

Lionel came to attention, saluted her smartly, and said in a low, rough-edged voice, 'Aye aye, sir! Midshipman Merry all present and correct, sir! What's our heading, sir? West, is it?'

'West,' said Rarty, striding off ahead of him. 'To the bridge.'

The bus came to a halt and the driver turned round. 'Mrs Boofus,' he said. A little louder: 'Mrs Boofus.'

She started, banging her knee against the seat in front. She had been deep in thought, staring through the window, but not seeing the quayside stop where she usually got off, and where the bus now stood. She felt uneasy; something wasn't right.

She stood up, red-faced and flustered, and almost ran to the front of the bus, where she mumbled a quick apology to Charlie without meeting his eye.

Impatient ferry passengers were already queueing for tickets as she opened up her kiosk, so she pushed her worries aside and got on with her work. When at last the queue had gone and all the passengers boarded, suddenly she had it: Rarty's shoes. Rarty had stopped to tie her shoelaces before going into school – but she didn't have any. Mrs Boofus remembered checking her new slip-ons before breakfast, to see if they were scuffed yet. Why on earth would she pretend to tie laces which weren't there?

'Egg-laying,' said Lionel.

'What?' asked Rarty. They had collected Rarty's old clothes from the shed, and bought some food on the way. Now they were walking north, towards the shore, having crossed the bridge. Rarty was trying to concentrate on the route to the dell, and was growing irritated at Lionel's interruptions.

'It means they lay eggs.'

'What does?'

'What you've got written on your hand.' Rarty looked down and remembered. Lionel put on Miss Fosby's voice. "Oviparous". Adjective. From the Latin *ovum*, egg. Reproducing by the laying of eggs.' Rarty was impressed. Lionel continued in his own voice. 'It's a good word – but why are you wearing it?'

'I saw it in a biology book. I didn't know what it meant, so I wrote it down. I was going to ask Mr Dawkins today.'

'What's so special about *this* word?'

'Nothing. It's a word, that's all.'

'But you must come across zillions of words every day. Why did you write this one down?'

'No reason. I just saw it and wondered.'

Lionel gave up. They walked on without speaking for a time. Rarty looked for the place where they had to turn left for the shore, while Lionel hummed absentmindedly beside her. Suddenly he stopped. 'You were reading about gumnors, weren't you? That's why you wrote it down.'

Rarty was beginning to realise that Lionel was sharp, however much he might play the clown. Even so, she didn't want to show him any hint of respect. 'She's not *a* gumnor,' she said crossly. 'She *is* Gumnor. It's her name.'

'I'm sorry. I didn't know.' They walked on in silence once more, over the tussocky grass towards the cliff-tops. Lionel could not contain his curiosity for long. 'What

49

sort of thing is it, then?' There was no reply. 'Sorry. Sorry. What sort of thing is *she*? What kind of animal?'

'A hugumnodin.'

'A what?' He asked her to spell it. 'Great word. Where's it from?'

'What do you mean? Words are just words. They don't come from anywhere.'

'Of course they do. That's etymology – knowing how words start off. Hugumnodin. It's not English, is it? It's strange. Who calls them that?'

'The island people. They speak a funny language – you must have heard them.'

Lionel nodded, but with a frown. He had heard the islanders talking with the city folk when they came ashore. Their accents were strong but they were speaking English. He had no idea they had a language all of their own. 'Do you know any islander words?'

'A few. My pa told me. He speaks islander. "Magarner" – that means fishing net. "Stroom" – boat.' She raised her leg in front of her. 'These are "durfers".'

'What – feet?'

'No, boots.'

'More. Tell me more.'

'I used to know more but I forgot them.' They had reached the cliff-top and were looking down on the shingle shore below. She pointed at the beach. 'That's a "clartey". If it was sand it would be a "scrasser". I remember those because that's what it sounds like when you walk on them.'

Lionel tried the words out under his breath, in time with his stride. 'Clartey. Clartey clartey clartey. Scrasser. Clartey scrasser clartey scrasser.' He smiled: she was right. He gazed beyond the beach to the ocean reflecting in silver sparkles the golden sun. 'And the sea? What do they call that?'

'They mainly call it Rua, like a name, but they have different words for it, if it's rough or stormy or calm. Calm is "haspar".' She paused, surprised that she knew these words. 'Why are you so interested in words, anyway?'

'I like them. I read a lot. There's hundreds of books where I live, but nobody else reads them any more. It's my job to read them and let the words out.' They were walking along the cliff path. He looked down at the jumbled rocks far below. '"Oblivion". There's one. Noun: the state of being forgotten. I save them from dusty oblivion.' A moment later he thought of another word – pompous – but didn't say it. Instead, to try and stop her thinking it too, he carried on. 'I saw "oviparous" on your hand and thought maybe you liked words as well.'

'Not as much as you. I just wanted to know what it

meant. I thought it was something to do with eating all different kinds of things, but it didn't make sense because Gumnor only ever eats fish.'

'That's "omnivorous".'

'I bet you only like the big words that no one else knows, so you can show off,' Rarty said, not really believing herself.

'Not true. "Misled", I like. It looks like you should say it differently. "Frannet", too. I like the way it sounds.'

'What's a frannet?'

'It's the bit you put between the widger and the dootles when you're building a puxley post.'

Was he making fun of her? Rarty couldn't tell from his face until she saw the corner of his mouth twitching. He looked away to hide it, but she hit him anyway. 'I'll puxley you,' she laughed. 'And when I'm done I'll widger your dootles.' He was laughing too, so she hit him again.

'Ouch!' he said, rubbing his arm. 'That one hurt.'

'Your punishment, Midshipman Merry, for having *misled* your captain.' He continued rubbing. 'I didn't hit you that hard,' she said.

'Maybe not, but I fear a *contusion* anyway. Noun: bruise, painful lump. You're stronger than you think, you know.'

* * *

52

On a similar cliff-top far to the south, Mr Boofus was also staring out to sea. He had paused to scan the rocks below for any sign of Gumnor when something offshore, some strange appearance of the sea, had caught his eye. Now he stood staring hard, holding his hand to his forehead to shield his eyes from the glare, trying to work out what it was.

The water was flat and calm, the sky bright, and the visibility good: he could just make out the harbour walls on Jetta, the nearest island, away to the north-west. The next island, Gallican, was fainter, being more distant, and it was near there that the sea looked odd. A mile off the southern tip was a patch where the water looked troubled. It seemed churned up, busy with movement. Everywhere else was calm, but here waves, spray and flashes of white all mixed together in a furious tumult.

Mr Boofus didn't understand. He had never seen anything like this before, in all his days at sea. He continued staring, trying to make it out, muttering to himself all the while. 'Well I'll be blowed. Strange it is. I hope there's no fishermen caught up in that. Proper odd it looks. I don't like it. I don't like it, no.'

Then, suddenly, a black shape rose up out of the water, thirty, forty, fifty feet and more, before crashing back down in a great cloud of foam and spray. 'A whale?'

he asked out loud. 'Surely not. Not here, at this time of year. Not that close to shore. And certainly not breaching like that. It can't be.' Whales regularly migrated along the coast, but they always kept well clear of the city, and even of the islands, revealing themselves to fishermen as a distant water-spout or a glimpse of tail fluke.

As he stared, disbelieving, another black shape, smaller than the first, leapt skywards from the raging sea. It seemed to hang motionless, straining upwards, before plunging back beneath the surface. Mr Boofus was astonished. 'Two of them! No wonder the water's all stirred up. It must be quite a sight up close.'

He was beginning to think that there was more disturbance than even two great whales could make, when he saw a sight that robbed him of all speech and motion. Together, very slowly, and with an awesome majesty, at least five great pairs of whale flukes appeared, soaring high above the water to be silhouetted against the sky. They rose in unison as the water boiled beneath, and far away though he was, Mr Boofus could feel the power throb within them for a frozen moment. The huge tails stood above the water like the masts of some strange sinking ship, giving a last salute. It seemed to Mr Boofus that everything else stopped too: the breeze in the grass, the calls of the gulls, the waves on the beach, even his own breathing. At last the moment ended, broken by further movement of all five tails, which thundered down against the water in a co-ordinated blow, five fingers in a massive fist. Mr Boofus felt, more than heard, the rumbling crash as they hit the surface. The power amazed and humbled him, and he took a step backwards. All around, squadrons of gulls rose from the cliffs in a writhing white cloud, startled at the sound and calling out in fear.

As he stared on, the water gradually settled, until it appeared as calm as the sea around it. Of the whales there was no sign. Mr Boofus waited until he was quite sure the spectacle was over, then moved on along the path. He was no longer searching properly. He was too distracted and troubled by what he had just seen. But he realised that it didn't matter. If Gumnor was to be found, it would not be here, but offshore, among the islands. He was convinced that the whale display was connected somehow to Gumnor's vanishing, although he could not say why.

Gallican, he said to himself, briskening his pace homeward. That's where she'll be. That's where we'll find her.

* * *

Mrs Flaggins was first down the gangway and, once ashore, made straight for the kiosk, where Mrs Boofus saw her coming and sighed. For most of the morning she had sold tickets politely and efficiently, while her troubles gnawed away like toothache. She really did not feel like talking to Mrs Flaggins. Not today.

Mrs Flaggins tottered up fast, all a-jabber from afar. 'Mrs Boofus, Mrs Boofus. I didn't expect to see you here. It must be terrible for you. You must be so worried.'

'Well, yes. Still no Gumnor, and there's only four days left.'

'No, no, no – I mean about Rarty.'

Mrs Boofus's worry about Rarty's shoes, seeded that morning, suddenly broke out in the full bloom of fear. Mrs Flaggins watched the tickets tremble in her hand.

'What do you mean? I took her to school today,' was all she could find to say. 'I took her to school.'

'She's not there now,' said Mrs Flaggins. She was taken aback by Mrs Boofus's distress, and tried hard to soften her tone. 'I saw her from the boat.'

'When?'

'Just now, on the way over. I had to go on deck for some air, the sea was that rough between Jetta and Gallican – very odd it was, more a swirl than a swell, but only in that place, and everywhere else glass smooth.

Something to do with the tides, I suppose.' Mrs Boofus breathed a long get-to-the-point sigh. 'Anyway, I was still on deck as we came under the bridge. I swear it was Rarty, walking away north, with a boy.'

'A boy?'

'I don't know him.'

'But going where?'

'I've no idea. She looked prepared, though. She had a rucksack with her, and that old hat of Lon's. That's how I knew her.'

'But I got her dressed for school.' Mrs Boofus was more and more distraught. 'I took her there. I watched her go in.'

'She wasn't in her uniform, that's for sure, and nor was that boy she was with.' She paused. 'I'm sorry, Mrs B. I thought you would know already.' For once Mrs Flaggins had little else to say. 'She's a smart lass – she can look after herself. She'll be all right, I'm sure. Perhaps she's gone off to look for Gumnor too.'

Mrs Boofus slumped down in the corner. She sat, staring with unseeing eyes at the piles of tickets for Gallican, Jetta, Honshaw, Murdo and the other islands. Mrs Flaggins jabbered on for a while, but when she saw that Mrs Boofus no longer heard her, she slipped away to the market.

Mrs Boofus tried to think clearly, to work out what to do. If Mrs Flaggins was right – a big if – her uneasiness over Rarty's shoelaces was confirmed and magnified. She can't have gone into school at all, she thought. No one will know she's missing. I have to tell them. She got up, put on her overcoat, and began locking up.

Outside, the noon ferry was making steam. The Murdo crabbers would soon be queueing for tickets. She couldn't just abandon the kiosk. She'd be letting so many people down – the customers, her boss, the ferrymen. She might lose her job, and if they failed to find Gumnor, Lon would lose his, and they'd have no home either. Her job might be the only support the family had.

She stood by the door, fiddling with the top button of her coat. She thought about Rarty, and fastened it; then about the kiosk, and undid it again, over and over. The choice facing her was simple but stark – her daughter or her job – and when at last she saw it that way, she knew it was no choice at all. She fastened her coat once more, scribbled a note for the kiosk window, and left.

CHAPTER FOUR
THE CLIFFS

RARTY LED LIONEL ALONG THE CLIFF-TOP
path until, as they neared the dell, she began to feel
uneasy. She squinted at the sun, and told him it was
time for lunch. They settled down in the long grass
beside the path, where Rarty unwrapped the bread,
cheese and apples they had bought on the way to the
bridge.

'How much further?' asked Lionel as he watched her
cut the bread.

'Not far. Look, you can see it.' She pointed out with
her knife the dell, visible as a gap in the cliff's edge just
half a mile away. 'From here we have to be careful. We
shouldn't really be here. There'll be big trouble if they
catch us.'

'I didn't see any notices.'

'It doesn't matter. They don't want people round here. Pa and me got towed away by the Navy, and there were loads of marines round here searching. Something funny happened here, and I reckon it's to do with Gumnor. That's why I – that's why *we* came.'

'But why not with your pa?'

She was silent for a while. 'I think he's . . .' she found it hard to say. 'I think he's scared. The Navy men frightened him. He didn't like me seeing that. So I couldn't say.'

Lionel looked at her. 'Weren't you frightened too?'

'Yes, but . . . but I told myself that if they were scary it could only mean something *must* have happened here. Pa's friend, John Quarrie, told us about marines searching all through the night, asking if he'd seen anything.'

'*Something* . . . maybe – but why to do with Gumnor?'

'Don't you see? The very same night she went missing there were all kinds of strange doings round here. It's too much of a . . . of a . . . what's the word?'

'Coincidence.' He lay back in the long grass, watching the seagulls watching him eat. 'You're pretty sure about this, aren't you?'

'Yes,' she said firmly, although she didn't feel it. She worried about what her teachers would say, and how her parents would react. It would be all right if she found

Gumnor, but if she didn't . . .

The gulls were getting bolder in their passes overhead. Lionel threw his apple core at one of them. He missed, but the bird behind caught it expertly and made off, closely pursued by three or four others screaming their determination to deny it the peace to eat.

The remaining birds came closer still, and Rarty too lay back to watch them. She had always been impressed by their flying skills, and loved the way they could stay aloft for ages, soaring effortlessly along the cliffs. She tossed up some crusts for them to catch, but immediately regretted the gully hubbub that followed.

'Don't feed them any more,' she said. 'The marines might see. We'll just lie quiet till they've gone.'

Lionel felt chilled, stretched out on the still-damp grass, and sat up to put on his jacket. Two nearby gulls suspected further food and moved in closer, hanging overhead. Lionel lay back, flung his arms out sideways, and twisted his head from side to side; an inverse imitation of the birds above. The gulls would lower one webbed foot to steer, or both to brake. Lionel copied them, raising his own feet and waggling them in the air. He even tried to mimic the cries they made, until Rarty shut him up.

'I wonder what we look like to them,' he said, trying

to make his eyes look beady.

'I know what you look like,' said Rarty. 'Some horrible reflection in a twisty mirror.'

He tried to imagine looking down on himself, reflected as a bird boy embedded in grass. 'Gulls are pretty horrible to begin with,' he said. 'They might be glad to think they look like this.'

'They are not horrible. They're all smooth and white, and they fly like . . . like . . . they fly like anything. You just watch them.'

Lionel gazed at his shoes in midair above him. 'I wish I had yellow feet,' he muttered.

Rarty didn't hear him. 'They look so smooth you can't tell they're made of feathers,' she said. 'You only see that if you can get above them.'

'Really?' Lionel wondered. He crawled to the cliff edge and looked down on the soaring seagulls. True enough, the feathers on the backs of their wings – but not, he noticed, on the backs of their bodies – were ruffled and lifted up to quiver, insubstantial, in the thin air. Why hadn't he seen this before? There were some things Rarty saw much better than he did.

One bird was having fun. It hovered before him, then dipped one wing and swept off to the right, in a great wheeling curve. The curve grew into a circle as it sped by, dodging the other birds, then it slowed and turned back into the wind to soar, stationary, in front of him once more, a seagull smile on its birdy face.

Lionel watched, entranced, as the gull did this again and again. On the third pass it seemed to catch his eye as he stared down – and on the fourth he thought it winked at him. Impossible, said a sensible voice somewhere inside. Birds don't wink.

It didn't matter. The bird made flight look so exhilarating, so easy, so free, that Lionel wanted to join in, in some small way. He stood up, right on the edge, his toes dangling over the giddy drop. He unbuttoned his jacket, and held it wide open with outstretched arms, to fill with air and billow in the breeze. He looked down at the jaggy rocks below, then at the smirking gull, and flung his head back to feel the wind. Lift me up, he thought. Lift me up and take me away. I want to fly. I really, *really* want to fly.

Suddenly he was disconnected from the ground and pulled sharply backwards. A thought flashed up – my wishes answered! – before he crashed down on the grass, in a tangle of arms and legs and crumpled jacket wings.

'You stupid boy,' hissed Rarty, her hand still grasping his belt. She was shaking and clearly very angry. 'You *stupid* boy.'

He was breathless from his fall, and astonished at her anger. He didn't think she'd worry about him like this. 'I wouldn't have fallen,' he said. 'The wind was holding me up.'

'Stupid,' she said again. She was frightened and angry and – yes – worried that he might have fallen. But most of all she was angry. 'I wouldn't care if you did fall, except for the noise you'd make.' He was finding it hard to look at her. She was angry like his mother got. 'Anybody could have seen you. We're supposed to be lying down quietly, out of sight. If anyone was looking up here because of the gulls they're bound to have seen you now.' She let go of his belt. 'I told you outside school, didn't I? Do as I say, remember?' Just like his mother. 'We've *got* to be careful here.'

'I'm sorry,' said Lionel quietly. 'I just wanted to feel I could fly for a while.' He looked up. 'Don't you ever wish you could?' Rarty shook her head, but he knew she did – everyone did. 'Have you ever tried?' She shook her head again. 'I fly in my dreams sometimes,' he said. His face lit up. 'It's *brilliant*.'

His remembered joy was so intense, his eyes so bright, that Rarty could not stay angry with him for long. 'Come on,' she said, 'there's no point lying here quietly now. Let's go on to the dell.'

Far below, John Quarrie tramped over the shingle beach – the clartey – collecting driftwood for his fire. He hadn't found much, and was about to turn back, when something fell out of the sky and splattered on the stones beside him.

A crab? he thought, hopefully. The gulls often dropped crabs on the stones here to break them open and get at the rich meat inside. If this was a big one, and not too smashed, it might make a nice meal later, if only he could find cookwood enough. His hunger panged hollow when he saw this was no crab at all, but an apple core, tooth-marked and fresh. He tossed it aside, and the gulls descended greedily to fight over it. John Quarrie frowned. 'Must be someone about,' he said to himself, looking round and seeing no one. 'They're keeping theyselves well hid.'

Fearing marines, he peered about more carefully and spotted a cliff-top commotion half a mile north, away towards the dell. 'What's all that, then?' he asked, this time out loud, his curiosity a-mingle with fear. He paused, then set off north, casting sly cliffward glances. 'Be *blowed* if they'll scare me off,' he muttered.

He'd not gone a furlong when an extraordinary sight brought him up short. Right on the cliff edge, teetering over the hundred-foot drop, stood a small, strange figure, with arms spread-eagled, head held high, and a pair of miniature makeshift wings flapping clumsily behind. John Quarrie watched, bewildered. A man? Too small. But surely not a child? As he watched, dreading a terrible fall, the figure vanished, jerked backwards and upwards, as if by invisible rope.

John Quarrie stared on, but saw no more than a fading flurry of gulls. 'Not a marine, at least.' He had to get up to the cliff-top, and the nearest rising path was at the back of the dell, so he dropped his scanty driftwood and strode off. 'All these doings, I don't know. Apple cores from the sky. Humph. Cliff-top birdmen what vanish in a trice. Whatever next? Is it just my old eyes? Or am I finally going mad?'

Mr Boofus recognised his wife long before she saw him. They were approaching their cottage from opposite directions. 'Ho!' he called, waving his arms. 'Ho there, Elna!'

She was too preoccupied to notice him at first, but as soon as she did she burst into tears and rushed into his embrace. 'Oh, Lon, Lon, it's terrible. First Gumnor, now Rarty,' she babbled. 'I don't know where she's gone, or what to do, or anything. It's too much.'

'What on earth –?' he tried to ask.

'Missing. She's missing, Lon, she's gone.' She sobbed heavily, encircled in his burly arms. 'I took her to school, like always. Then, mid-morning, that Jinty Flaggins saw her. Walking over the bridge, she was, no uniform, with a boy. They've run away, the two of them. But where? And why?' She broke down again.

'Slow down, love, slow down. You're going too fast for me.' He led her to the garden gate. 'Come on in and tell me slowly so I understand.'

He shepherded her into the kitchen where he pieced together the story of Rarty's disappearance, broken up as it was by Elna's fits of weeping and his attempts to console her.

'She planned it, you say. Mmmmm. It seems so, with the clothes and that,' he muttered, staring at the empty hearth. 'Heading north, was she? No one up there she knows.' He got up to set the fire, needing to keep his hands busy while he pondered. The kindling soon caught, and he was rattling coal from the scuttle when he remembered. 'Yes she does.' He stood up and turned to his wife. 'John Quarrie. She met him when we were up there hunting Gumnor. I'll wager she's gone a-searchin' for Gumnor herself. She's not run away, love.' He placed a hand on Elna's shoulder.

'She'll be home tonight. I'm sure of it.'

'But what shall we do till then, Lon?' She looked up sharply. 'I thought there'd be no one here when I got back. I didn't expect you so soon, Lon.' Her eyes narrowed. 'You haven't found Gumnor, have you? She's not . . . You haven't . . .'

'No, love, I haven't, not dead nor alive. And neither will we on these shores – but I know where she'll be. Let's you and I busy up packin' for the islands till Rarty's back, love. We've an early start on the morrow, and there's clothes and vittles and gifts for Gallicaners to stow.'

CHAPTER FIVE
TRAPPED

THE DELL, CREATED BY A LANDSLIP YEARS ago, was now a semi-circular clutter of rocky outcrops, separated by steep slopes, with piles of boulders strewn between. Scrawny gorse bushes grew wherever they could gain a hold. There were awkward crevices and hidden crannies everywhere. Rarty sighed. It would take a long time to search. Still, they had to start somewhere. She directed Lionel to the right while she took the left. They would start at the top and work down.

After a while Rarty paused to watch Lionel clambering about opposite her. He was not agile, and she saw no system in his searching. He reminded her of a lost insect, spidering about at random. I suppose he's *some* help, she thought, turning back to the rocks before her. And at least he's doing no harm.

There was a loud clatter. She looked around to see a large stone bouncing down among the outcrops. Lionel, who had dislodged it, stood dismayed, unable to meet her eye. They both watched the stone, which had knocked free some others in its fall, until it came to a halt. The echoes rattled around the dell, then died away, and the dust quickly dispersed in the breeze.

John Quarrie heard the racket and stepped out into the open at the bottom of the dell, gazing upwards. All he could make out was a pair of small people ('It *is* children.'); and they could only see one large person ('A marine? We're for it now.'). The three of them froze, statue-still, then snapped into motion, John Quarrie striding forwards up the rock-strewn slopes, while Rarty and Lionel scrambled for shelter. Rarty had no idea where she was going – she just ran, her rucksack thumping on her back to match the heart in her chest. Gorse branches snagged her clothes and tugged at her hair, and one, higher than the rest, whipped across her face with a vicious swish. She was surprised there was no pain.

Underfoot, gorse roots tangled amid scattered stones, and threatened to trip her up or turn her ankle. She told herself to go slower, to watch her footing, but just as she looked down, the ground beneath her vanished completely. A dark crevice gaped upwards like a rocky mouth, hungry for her. Instinctively, she grabbed at a nearby gorse branch, but it came away in her hand, and she plunged into the jaws of the earth, bumping against the sides, as she fell deep into increasing darkness. She scrabbled wildly, trying to catch the dim rocky ledges as they passed. Ten, twenty, thirty feet – how much further? At last she came to an abrupt and juddering halt, wedged tightly between the damp, dark walls. Stones, soil and branches of gorse bush continued to fall around her for a while; but soon everything was still and silent once more, except for her heaving chest and the rasp of her breathing.

If I'm breathing I must be alive, she thought, not sure whether to believe it. At first she didn't dare move, in case she had done some serious damage. The pain of multiple cuts and bruises soon made itself felt as she lay there, trembling and scared, but at least there didn't seem to be any big pains.

She wriggled herself free a little, and tentatively moved one limb at a time. 'This arm . . . yes . . . seems all right . . . now the other . . . good.' She ran her fingers over her head and face. There was a big lump on one temple, and something sticky – blood – running down her right cheek. Her nose and mouth were fine, and she could move her neck without pain. 'Good so far . . .' She could bend forwards and twist, although her ribs hurt all down one side. 'Now the legs.' One, her right, was bent up awkwardly beneath her. She could feel all the way down the shin, over the bruises and raw areas, to her foot. That's all right too, she thought.

She tried to push herself up by straightening her leg, but nothing happened. She tried again, harder. Still nothing. It wasn't her right leg that was the problem, but the left. It was stretched out straight below her, and would not move at all. She could bend far enough to reach the knee, but no further. She felt a surge of panic. Stuck down here, trapped, with a broken leg . . . she thought.

She struggled to stay calm. 'Think it through,' she told herself out loud, and was startled by the echo. 'If it was broken it would hurt. More than this. So it's not broken. Just stuck.' And it was – stuck fast, jammed in the crevice, and held there by the pile of stones she had brought down with her. She was in a fix.

She tried a long, steady pull, but her leg would not budge; and then a sudden sharp jerk, but that only hurt. She tried wiggling her foot, and pulling and pushing and twisting, but it was no use. Nothing worked. She bent forward again. If I can clear some of these stones I might get it free. She pushed aside the first few rocks, but they tumbled straight back into place. She could only hold one or two at a time, and there were no ledges nearby to move them to. She straightened up, feeling the panic rise within her again. She tried hard to control her breathing, taking deeper, slower breaths, but this made her ribs hurt more, especially where the rucksack straps dug in. As she struggled to loosen them an idea was born. 'Of course,' she said.

She slid the rucksack off her back, placed it by her knee, and began to fill it with the rocks which pinned her leg in place. She soon felt her leg loosening, although the rucksack was filling fast. These last two, she thought. That should do it. The last rock was strange. It was bigger than the others, though not as heavy. It was not cold and damp and sharp-edged, like the rest, but smooth, and mossy and almost warm. She put it in her rucksack with the others, and tried once more to free her leg. Now at last she could move her ankle, and even her toes. She pulled gently and her ankle popped free. Rarty held her breath, bending down to feel for the jagged points of bone she feared, then let out a long deep sigh. Her leg was bruised and sore and already swelling fast – but it was not broken.

She looked up. The ragged crack of light marking the

entrance to the crevice seemed very far away. She might not be stuck any more, but it was going to be a long, hard climb in the dark before she could get out. She thought about calling for help, but decided against, at least for now. She might want to be rescued, but not by marines. She wondered about Lionel. Had he been caught? What had he told them?

She emptied her rucksack of all the rocks except the strange one, which she wanted to inspect in the light. She swung it on to her back and set about clambering up towards the surface far above. There were few good handholds but down here, where the crevice was narrow, she could bridge between the walls. Her climbing was slow and deliberate, and she had to feel for each new hold in the dense darkness.

'At least if I can't see it won't matter if I look down.' About halfway up she paused for a rest, and looked up again, glad to see the fissure opening out to let in more light. For a moment she thought she saw some movement overhead. She stared hard, rubbing the dust from her eyes, but everything was still, and all she could hear was the breeze in the gorse bushes which overhung the lips of the crevice like a prickly moustache. She carried on up.

The climbing was more difficult now that the crevice

was widening, because she had to choose one side and could no longer alternate between them. Her fingers, rubbed raw by her scrabbling when she fell, were painful and stiff, and she was getting shaky with tiredness and shock. There were no safe ledges for rest, so she had to keep moving on up. Close to the top she slipped and nearly fell. She knew she had to climb faster, whatever the risk, because she was so tired she didn't think she could hold on much longer. Her heart was pounding and her lungs strained. Sweat mingled with the blood running down her cheek. Her fingers hurt to numbness, so that her feeling for the handholds was fading fast.

'Climb. Just climb,' she told herself. 'Don't look down, only up. Push on now or you'll never get out. Come *on*.'

Her strength had almost gone when she finally got one hand over the lip of the crevice. She paused, feeling for a hold – and a large rough hand enclosed her wrist in an unforgiving grasp. She looked up, wild-eyed and blinking in the now-bright light. All she could see was the outline of two heads, one large, one small, peering down at her. There was a whiff of fish. After all her efforts she had been caught, but by now she was too tired to mind.

She recognised John Quarrie's gruff voice the instant

he spoke. 'Come on, now. I've got you. You're safe.' He hauled her up, as if reeling in a lobster, and laid her gently on the ground. She could see the concern in his weather-beaten face as he bent over her, and she was dimly aware of Lionel, standing behind him, silent and awkward. 'Oh my,' said John Quarrie. 'Oh my. Look at you. Are you hurt?'

Rarty shook her head. Tears of relief and pain welled up in her eyes, and her throat closed up so she could not speak. She shook her head again but could hold back no longer and began to cry. Lionel stepped back while John Quarrie comforted her. When her sobbing had stopped he handed Lionel her rucksack and bid him follow. He gingerly picked her up and set off towards his cottage, pretending not to notice the damp patch her tears made on his shoulder.

'More hot water, lad,' said John Quarrie. A driftwood fire crackled in his hearth, a pan of water bubbling above it. Rarty, in vest and shorts, sat by the table, all her bruises now displayed. With the dirt and blood cleaned away she looked better than when she'd emerged from the earth. John Quarrie wiped the last of the blood from her cheek to reveal two shallow horizontal scratches from nose to cheekbone. He touched them gently. 'Red Indian marks these,' he said to her, and then, turning to Lionel, 'Look sharp now, lad, look sharp.'

Lionel was already feeling stupid because John Quarrie had caught him so quickly, and because he'd been useless at finding or helping Rarty, but he resented this cabin-boy treatment. All he was fit for was fetching hot water, it seemed, and he'd already scalded himself doing that. He felt sorry for Rarty, but couldn't help blaming her too. What did she go jumping down holes for? And coming up like some battered troll dragged from its cave?

He carried another steaming bowl to the table, muttering under his breath. 'Troll? Goblin, maybe. Leprechaun, perhaps. Wailed like a banshee – no, a *mandrake* – when we pulled her from the earth.' He put the bowl down. 'Trolls, pah!' Rarty looked up.

'What was that?' asked John Quarrie tetchily.

'Nothing, Mr Quarrie,' said Lionel. (Trollmaster, he thought.) 'More water?'

'Yes, and we'll need something for bandages. That towel there – I think it's clean.'

Lionel turned away, his face distorting into a hideous scowl. He affected a grotesque hunchback walk, dragging one leg behind him. 'Yeth, mathter,' he lisped softly. 'Oh yeth. The bandageth. Can we tie her up and put her with the other trollth? Can we, mathter, pleathe?'

Rarty watched him over John Quarrie's shoulder. She began to giggle. 'I'm right glad that flow of tears be stemmed, lass,' said John Quarrie. 'But it beats me what you have to laugh over.'

'Sorry, Mr Quarrie.' She looked down as he inspected her ankle to avoid catching Lionel's eye.

John Quarrie straightened up. 'No breaks, I think. But this ankle and those ribs are proper bashed up and want strappin'.' He ripped the towel in half, lengthways, and gave one part to Lionel. 'Here, lad, tear this up for me. In strips, mind.'

Lionel nodded and stepped back from the table, taking care that Rarty, but not John Quarrie, could still see him. He resumed his scowl, now worse than before. One eye bulged out and his tongue lolled horribly from his mouth. He bent like a crab, bony elbows splayed wide, tugging at the cloth. 'Yeth, mathter. Rip and tear, yeth.' He ground his teeth, enjoying the noise as the first strip came away. 'Oh good, yeth. Thith ith good, mathter. Shredding, I am. Rending and cleaving.' Another strip tore off. His breathing was getting noisy. 'More of thith, mathter, more rending, yeth. I'm ripping yarn, heh heh heh.'

Rarty's giggles were building to a full-throated laugh when the door burst open and two burly marines rushed in, bristling with guns and truncheons.

'ON THE FLOOR!' one shouted.

None of them moved.

'NOW!' yelled the other, waving his gun.

All three of them threw themselves down.

'HANDS ON YOUR HEADS! NOBODY MOVE!'

Rarty and Lionel looked at each other, wide-eyed with fear. More marines stomped into the cottage.

'At ease, corporal,' said a voice Rarty thought she knew. 'At ease, all. Shoulder arms, safety on.' The first two marines stepped back and swung their guns aside. 'Commendable enthusiasm, corporal, but a little misplaced. An old man and two children.' Rarty *did* know this voice. 'No danger, you see.'

'Yessir. Sorry, sir,' said the first marine. He sounded disappointed.

'Up you get,' said the familiar voice. Again none of them moved, though Rarty did turn to look at him. It was the officer from the patrol boat. 'It's all right. You can get up now. My corporal is a little emphatic in his methods, that's all.'

They stood up slowly, brushing away the dust of the floor from their clothes, and nervously eyeing the guns.

'Now you'd be Quarrie, yes?' demanded the officer.

'That's Mr Quarrie to you.'

'Yes, yes, of course. Mr Quarrie. I must say –'

'And I don't take kindly to men with guns bursting in on my 'ome nor orderin' me about neither.'

'No. As I said, a little emphatic.' He was getting irritated at this grizzled fisherman and his obstinacy. 'Now, we've had reports –'

'Emphatic be blowed. I will 'ave a 'pology from you now or from your seniors later.' Rarty was impressed.

The officer sighed. 'Very well. I apologise, *Mr* Quarrie for the way we have disturbed you.' There was nothing sorry in the way he said it.

Even so, John Quarrie was satisfied: he had won. 'Now, what is it you want?' he asked, to emphasise that it was he who was in control.

'We're seeking two children reported missing. It seems we've found them.' Rarty was surprised they were being looked for so soon.

'No you ain't. *I* found 'em. One of them is 'urt, and I were tending 'er when you burst in. I'll carry on, if it's all the same to you.' He motioned to Rarty to sit down and set about strapping her ankle again, smiling warmly to reassure her.

'Miss Boofus, isn't it?' asked the officer, towering over

her. She nodded. 'We met offshore, I believe, not long ago. You were with your father.' She nodded again. 'You didn't speak then either. Perhaps you could tell me how, and more importantly *where* you acquired those wounds.'

Rarty stared at him, not knowing what to say. John Quarrie spoke for her. 'Not far from here. She'd fallen at the cliffs.'

'North or south of here?' asked the officer casually.

'South,' John Quarrie lied firmly. He knew they could all have been arrested for entering the dell. The officer was looking at Rarty. She met his gaze steadily and nodded once more.

'And you didn't see anything out of the ordinary in your wanderings?' She shook her head. It was hard to tell if he believed her or not. His sea-coloured eyes were looking deep into her. 'What was it you were doing up here anyway, young lady?'

''Er and 'er friend were bunkin' off school to look for their 'ugumnodin,' John Quarrie broke in again and, because the officer looked blank, he added, 'the foghorn beast.'

At last the officer stopped staring at Rarty and turned his attention to Lionel. 'And you would be?'

'Lionel Merry,' said John Quarrie, who was doing his best to protect them from this interrogation. 'Known 'ereabouts as Igor,' he said, winking at Lionel, who stood aghast. John Quarrie must have heard every word of his hunchback performance. Rarty sniggered at this. The officer, increasingly irritated, snapped back at her, 'Do you know how many people are looking for you, my girl? Us, the police, your teachers, your family, hunting all over. It's not a laughing matter. We have already wasted quite enough time on this searching. Now come with us.'

Rarty's smile vanished. 'Go with you where?' asked John Quarrie. Perhaps they were to be arrested after all.

'Home, of course,' said the officer. 'Where else?'

'If it's 'ome they're going, then 'tis I who'll take 'em,' said John Quarrie. 'I know 'er father well.'

'Very well,' said the officer, 'but let those bruises be a lesson to you and your friend, young lady. This is a dangerous place and much of it is forbidden. If we find you here again you will not be going home quite so soon.' He led his men out of the cottage and away to their jeep parked nearby. Rarty, Lionel and John Quarrie watched them go, then all three let out a big deep breath together.

'I'm sorry about the Igor business, Mr Quarrie,' said Lionel, awkwardly, but John Quarrie wouldn't have it. 'No matter, lad, no matter. I like a little spirit in a boy. This 'ere lass has plenty and I'm glad to see you 'ave some too. Now come on, let's be on our way.'

CHAPTER SIX
A LIVING GHOST

'YOU MEAN YOU'VE LIVED IN DALMOUTH ALL your life and you've never been to the islands?' asked Rarty. The wind was playing with her hair as she and Lionel stood in the bows, watching Jetta pass to starboard.

Lionel shook his head. 'I've never been on a ferry,' he said, leaning over the rail to watch the bow wave as it boiled beneath. 'I didn't know they could go so fast.' The shock of cold salt spray on his face made him step back abruptly, laughing. 'Come on. Show me round.' She was surprised to find him taking her hand.

She led him along the starboard rail to the sun-deck at the stern. Her parents and John Quarrie sat on a bench nearby, talking with a quiet intensity. At their feet lay two battered suitcases, a naval kitbag, and a wicker food basket.

'You mustn't upset yourself so, Elna,' said Mr Boofus.

'He didn't need to be so harsh,' she replied, close to tears. A piece of paper fluttered in her hand like a restless pigeon. 'Has he no children of his own?'

'You don't need wains yourself to know the hold they have on a parent's care,' said John Quarrie, quietly eyeing Rarty and Lionel as they stood at the stern rail, either side of the flag.

Mrs Boofus looked up. 'Bless you, John, I was so glad to have Rarty back last night that I clean forgot to thank you right. I –'

He held up his hand to stop her. 'No matter, Elna, no matter. You showed me your thanks with your food and board, and welcome both were. Besides, it cheered me greatly too, to see 'em home, safe and sound.' He paused. 'Though your lass weren't quite so sound as when she left, eh?'

A crewman approached. 'Mrs Boofus,' he said. She knew his windburnt face, but not his name. 'I want you to know that, though it were a bother, us doin' the tickets yest'day, with your kiosk closed an' all, me an' the rest of the crew here do understan'.' Mrs Boofus looked up to see a smile where she had feared a frown. 'Even if our guv'nor don't,' the sailor added. 'I seen him goin' on at you when you boarded just now. I heard some o' what he said. It weren't called for.' She tried to smile back and find words to thank him, but none would come.

Mr Boofus stepped in. He held out his hand. 'You're a good man, Jonas. All of you are. You have our thanks.'

Jonas shook hands and returned to his duties on the bridge above. Mr Boofus turned to his wife. 'You see, Elna? It's only him back there who don't understand. Now let's get rid of that paper, eh?' He took the fluttering sheet, screwed it up and tossed it into a waste bin nearby.

Lionel was curious to know what was on the paper, but was diverted by Rarty's yelling nudges. 'There! There's one! D'you see?' she said.

He followed her outstretched arm, squinting in the low sun. He shook his head. All he could see was water.

'Another!' She was shouting now.

He looked harder, and then at last he saw them: a platoon of round seal heads with liquid eyes and black snub noses, bobbing in the water between the waves, like helmeted soldiers peering over trench parapets. Their stare was watchful and wary, as if they were sentries; and in a way they were, for behind, on a collection of bleak rocks marked by a warning buoy, other seals basked their bellies in the October sun. The sentry seals would disappear, one at a time, then bob up again nearby, still staring, as if to make sure the ferry – friend or foe? – was moving on.

Lionel stared back, blinking. A sudden mischievous urge prompted him to climb up and stand precariously on the stern rail, clutching the flagpole in one hand. With the other he grasped the flag and furled it round his shoulders. 'Long live the King!' he yelled at the seals with an extravagant gesture. 'Long live His Majesty!'

Rarty was mystified. 'Don't you see?' said Lionel, jumping down. 'They're Roundheads. And me, I'm a Cavalier.' She still didn't follow. 'Oliver Cromwell? The Civil War?' he ventured. She shook her head. He explained as much as he could remember for what remained of their voyage.

'How do you know all this?' she asked, as the ferry slowed in its approach to the little harbour at Gallican.

'I told you – I read a lot. They leave me to myself, and where I live there's books everywhere. No one else but me bothers with them now. I could show you them sometime if you like.'

'Yes. I'd like that,' she said vaguely, her attention drawn to a gathering on the quayside.

Her lack of interest in his home life upset Lionel, though he tried not to let it show. Surely she knows it's lonely? he thought. He didn't want to join Rarty's inspection of the welcome party, and looked round for something else to do. The rubbish bin was nearby,

and he rummaged in it for the paper Mr Boofus
had discarded.

He crouched down to smooth out the crumpled note
and tried to decipher the shaky writing. It wasn't until
he remembered Mrs Boofus's grumpy boss tearing it off
the kiosk window that he understood – it was the note
she'd written the day before, when she'd left her job to
look for him and Rarty. He read it through:

Sorry, closed
Urgent famly
~~business~~ bisiness.
Please by tickits
on bord ferry.
Sorry for
inconvenence.

He reread it, finding his eye drawn back again and again
to the phrase 'Urgent family business', and wondering if
his own mother would have done the same.

Rarty shook his shoulder. 'Lionel?' she asked. He
seemed different somehow. 'Lionel, we've docked.'

He stood up abruptly, slid the crumpled paper into his
pocket, and saluted her. 'Aye aye, cap'n,' he said. The
faraway look in his eyes had gone. 'Midshipman Merry
at your service.'

* * *

Rarty surveyed the odd little group assembled on the quayside below. At its centre was a grey-bearded old man, who sat with an intense stillness about him in a home-made wooden wheelchair. There were two well-built younger men, whom Rarty could not tell apart, in seamen's garb. One held the wheelchair, his powerful hands resting lightly on the frame, the other stood to the left. On the other side was an elderly woman in a heavy overcoat. Wisps of grey hair peeked out beneath her brightly patterned headscarf. Two dark-eyed dogs sat in front, quietly watchful as the ferrymen swung the gangwalk on to the shore. They seemed to be waiting for someone to walk down it.

Mr Boofus stepped ashore first, followed by his wife and John Quarrie. He walked straight towards the waiting group, extending his hand to the man in the wheelchair. 'Waldo,' he said. 'It's been a long time.' The man in the wheelchair met his eyes briefly and nodded while his hand was shaken, but he said nothing.

The woman in the headscarf embraced Mr Boofus. 'Too long,' she said with a sigh. 'Too long by far.' She put a hand on Waldo's shoulder. 'He knew you would come today. I don't know how.'

'He's been watching that vessel with his spyglass since

she came under the bridge, Mr Boofus,' said the young man behind the wheelchair. 'He was so sure.' They too shook hands.

'You look well, Jeb. You an' Will both. Just boys you were last time I seen you. Men now.'

'Younger'n boys last time for me,' broke in John Quarrie. 'But I'd know you anywhere.' Will and Jeb looked uncertain and exchanged puzzled glances.

'You might not know him by sight, but you'll know his name, sure enough,' said Mr Boofus. 'This here's John Quarrie.'

The two young men were impressed. 'We used to hear a lot about you, Mr Quarrie, from Pa here,' said Jeb, indicating Waldo. 'Of course that was all . . . before.' He looked away and his voice trailed off.

As the greetings continued, Rarty held back, watching Waldo. The ice light in his eyes softened when her father and John Quarrie flanked his wheelchair. Her father summoned her and crouched alongside as she stood before the wheelchair. It felt like she was being presented to a king on his throne. 'Rarty, this is Mr Waldo McFee. A seafaring mate of mine and John's from days long gone. And these good people' – he waved his arm – 'are his family.' They smiled at Rarty, but she didn't notice. She was looking at Waldo, but he was looking *through* her, his slate-grey gaze unwaveringly fixed on the horizon. People and things in front of him were a distraction.

'Pleased to meet you,' said Rarty hesitantly, holding out her hand. He was right in front of her but she wondered if she could reach him, he seemed so far away. They shook hands, but the contact brought him no closer. It was like touching a living ghost, though she was more curious than frightened. His stare was so persistent she felt compelled to look over her shoulder, even though she knew the quayside was empty.

Mrs McFee saw this. 'Who's your friend, my dear?' she asked to ease Rarty's discomfort. Lionel stepped up to say hello, and the introductions were complete.

Jeb turned the wheelchair round, and they followed him along the quayside. 'You'll be over for Gumnor, then?' he said. Mr Boofus nodded. 'Will an' me'll help. We've our boat there to circle Gallican, maybe Jetta too.' He indicated a battered fishing boat moored in front of the ferry. She was showing her age but her paintwork was bright, and nowhere more so than in her name: *Colleen*.

As they passed her, Will spoke to his brother. 'I'll get 'er ready, Jeb,' he said, dropping down a ladder on to the deck, where he stepped over the nets and lobster pots to unlock the wheelhouse. Behind her, Rarty heard a clatter, then a cough, then a roar, as the *Colleen*'s engine started up. She turned to see a small cloud of thin blue smoke rising from the stern. The engine settled into a steady throb, the cloud cleared, and Will busied himself on deck. He saw her staring, and waved briefly. She waved back, but he had already returned to his work.

'Come along, Rarty,' called her mother, but in a kindly voice, for she knew Rarty was hobbled by her injuries.

The dogs sensed it too, for they dropped back to shepherd her along like a sickly lamb. Every few yards one or the other would look up at her with impassive deep brown eyes. When the darker dog to her right did this again she patted it on the nose. 'Where are you taking me?' she asked.

'It's not far,' said Mrs McFee. They were climbing steeply up from the harbour, on a narrow cobbled street. Mrs McFee stopped outside the last of a row of cottages, which were strung along the hillward side, overlooking the harbour below. 'Here we are,' she said to Rarty, while holding the gate open for Jeb and Waldo.

Rarty inspected the outside of the cottage as the others trooped in. It was larger than the others in the row, but its windows were still small, like eyes half-closed against a winter wind. There was an extra window on the ground floor, which looked newer. Where the others were square and shuttered, this was round, like a porthole. Through it she glimpsed brass.

The door opened straight into the front room. Jeb manoeuvred Waldo's chair into position between the porthole and the fire. Beside him was a small table covered with charts and navigating instruments and in front, on the windowsill, was the telescope. Without a word Waldo took it up, and turned to the porthole. Over his shoulder, Rarty could see that the little window offered a view of the harbour and its approaches and, beyond, Jetta, the mainland, and the great bridge, glowing gold in the sunlight. She stepped closer to try and identify the charts.

'Don't get too curious, Rarty,' said her father. 'We're just dropping these bags and heading straight back out.'

'Plenty o' time to look round later,' said Mrs McFee.

Their luggage deposited, Mr Boofus and John Quarrie made for the door, led by Jeb. Lionel and Rarty followed, but Mrs Boofus hesitated.

'Not you, Elna,' said Mrs McFee. 'You stay behind with me. I've something to show you.'

The dogs followed Lionel out of the door. He wasn't sure whether they were supposed to, and tried to close the garden gate on them. ''S all right, lad,' said Jeb. 'They loves boats, these two. They'll come with us.'

As they left, Rarty looked back. She could see Waldo through the porthole, intently scanning the horizon with his spyglass.

The *Colleen* left harbour with a dog on each beam, forelegs on the handrail, ears streaming in the wind. Lionel looked from one to the other, admiring their glossy coats and recalling his own exhilaration at the ferry's bows not long before.

'What d'you call them?' he asked Will, who was stacking lobster pots beside him. Will straightened and pointed at the light-coloured dog on the right. 'That's Port,' he said. 'And the other one's Starboard.' At the mention of their names each dog looked briefly back towards them.

Lionel was puzzled. He held out his hands in turn, clenching the fists and muttering in an effort to dredge up some submerged fact from deep within his memory. 'But I thought –'

'I know.' Will anticipated him. 'They're on the wrong sides. When they were pups they allas stood light coat to port, dark to starboard. Don't ask me why. Couldn't think of no names for 'un, so Port an' Starboard stuck.' A glimmer of a smile cracked his weathered face. 'They switch about now an' then to confuse visitors.'

'They're great,' said Lionel. He liked the dogs better now he knew their names. 'Do they always come with you?'

Will nodded and returned to his stacking. "Cept when we know it'll be rough. Ever seen a seasick dog?' Lionel shook his head. 'Not a pretty sight.'

As they pulled away from the harbour the cottages and crofts strung along the water's edge thinned out and fell away behind them, and the shoreline grew more rugged. Rarty studied the rocks as they rose and merged into forbidding cliff faces, interrupted here and there by almost-hidden coves. Jeb stepped out of the wheelhouse to hand a battered telescope to Lionel and some newer binoculars to Rarty.

'Your young eyes will be best behind these,' he said as he retook the helm. 'I'll take her as close to shore as I dare, but there's rocks aplenty to steer well clear of. You just keep scanning for your beast or any sign of her, an' pipe up loud at anything odd.'

Rarty and Lionel took up position on the port rail. Will went on working on the foredeck and, in the stern, Mr Boofus and John Quarrie stared blankly shorewards, occasionally exchanging a few quiet words. Lulled by the sound of the engine and the lack of activity on board, the dogs soon settled down to sleep, curled up in the bows like living ropes.

In this way they passed the rest of the morning. There was much to see. Flocks of terns hung over the water, cliff-top high. One by one they folded their wings and plunged abruptly waterwards, raising sharp plumes of spray as they broke the surface in search of the harvest beneath. Seals patrolled in twos and threes, sharing the fish feast from below, while raucous gulls wheeled low overhead, anxious for any scraps. Ashore, on the beaches, lay the bleached skeletons of long-dead trees, swept down the coast by the currents and washed up here by the tide. But no Gumnor. No sign she had ever been there. Nothing.

By the time they were halfway round the island, conversation had grown sparse, and disappointment hung over the *Colleen* like a blanket of fog. If they couldn't find Gumnor here, then where else could they look? Rarty didn't want to think these thoughts and kept scanning the shore till her eyes hurt. She found her attention drawn to another beach, bigger than the others, where the dead trees, instead of being scattered about, were piled up above the high watermark in a tangled wall some four feet tall.

She nudged Lionel. 'Look,' she said, but there was no need, for he had already seen it.

'It's like it was put there,' he said, 'to shelter behind or something.' Pictures from his father's books on ancient battles sprang into his head. 'It's like a barricade.' There was a word he was struggling for. 'Or a stockade.' No, he thought, too much cowboys-and-Indians. 'A palisade, maybe?' Closer, but still not right. What *was* that word?

'Logger's Strand, we calls it,' said Will, who had overheard Lionel's mutterings. 'Free firewood for all.' He explained how trees from the logging work in the great forests up the coast sometimes broke free. When the rivers were in spate they swept the trees out to sea, where the currents took them southwards along the coast for winter storms to cast ashore. Something about the currents and the tides funnelled them on to this particular beach. 'You can't land a boat hereabouts, and it's a bit of a hike from home,' said Will. 'But it's well worth it for winter warming.'

The two women climbed steadily uphill from the McFees' cottage. Near the top Mrs McFee paused, as if for breath, and swept her arm across the panorama before them.

'A fine sight, eh?' she declared, and it was. Far below, over the wrinkled rooftops of the houses on the hill, snugged the harbour, with the ferry still tied up and fishing boats bobbing at anchor. Beyond it swirled the Gallican Narrows, then Jetta, lying low in the sun-sparkled sea, like a tired whale warming its back. The dimmer outlines of other islands lay scattered in the background and then, almost lost in the thickening haze, the long low smudge that was the mainland.

'It *is* lovely,' said Mrs Boofus uncertainly. Surely Mrs McFee hadn't brought her up here simply for the view?

'Worth the climb?' Mrs Boofus nodded. "Tis the finest view on Gallican. Perhaps on all the islands.' Mrs McFee turned round. Set back from the road and almost hidden by an overgrown hedge was a cottage, now clearly abandoned. 'The folk as lived here loved it. They're long gone now, of course.'

Mrs Boofus peered over the hedge. The garden had reverted to Nature, who celebrated her victory in a riot of weeds and waist-high grass. The cottage appeared to float on a sea of green, like a derelict ship in a breaker's yard. The whitewash was stained and the plasterwork cracked. Some shutters and roof tiles were missing, and here and there spiders had done their cobweb best to shield the broken windowpanes.

'Let's have a look inside, shall we?' said Mrs McFee, pushing against the garden gate. The hedge held it fast, and the hinges were rusted tight so, try as she might, it would not budge. 'Come on, Elna. Give me a hand!' she puffed.

Mrs Boofus stood back, a puzzled frown on her face. Mrs McFee pulled a key from her apron pocket and waved it in front of her like a charm. 'It's all right, Elna, we're allowed.' Mrs Boofus, still hesitant, joined her in her struggle. With the two of them pushing, the gate opened so suddenly that they stumbled into the overgrown garden within. Small creatures scurried away unseen in fright.

'This is old Ma Tooley's place,' said Mrs McFee, dusting herself down. 'You must remember her.' Mrs Boofus didn't, but she nodded anyway.

'Leastways, it *was* her place. She died three winters past. There was a son, but he left for the city years before when her husband was still alive.' Mrs McFee looked under the hedge. 'Aha!' She took up an old stick she clearly knew was there and began beating at the grass with vigorous swishes to clear a path to the front door.

'Not a word from him since. No one knows where he is – *swish* – He prob'ly don't even know his old mother's no more.' Mrs Boofus followed, careful to keep her distance, but eager to hear the story.

'When she fell ill Ma begged me to take the keys and look after the place as best I could. Loved it she did –

swish – and she had it so pretty an' all.' They had reached the front door. Mrs McFee lay down the stick. 'It pains me to see it like this, it does. I do what I can, an' Will 'n' Jeb patch up winders an' roof each winter, but . . . well, you can see.'

While Mrs McFee brushed aside the cobwebs and fumbled with the key, Mrs Boofus looked round. Despite all the signs of neglect, there was something about the house, something she liked. It felt friendly, warm and welcoming, as if impatient to be lived in again. She found herself smiling.

Mrs McFee swung open the door, and they stepped inside. A dry mustiness replaced the fresh smells of the garden. The dust they raised hung in the still air, glinting gold in the shafts of sunlight which streamed through the windows and the holes in the roof. 'It's always light and airy in here,' she said, 'even in winter.'

She took Mrs Boofus on a tour of the rooms, talking all the while. 'It's not the only house standin' vacant on these islands, but to my mind it's the best. If someone don't move in soon, it'll start to fall apart, like all the others.' She opened the door to the kitchen, where a huge stone hearth gaped before them. Mrs Boofus eyed the array of racks and pot-hooks. They were rusty, but all still in place.

'There's space enough here to cook for a whole ship's crew,' she said, impressed.

'Aye,' replied Mrs McFee. 'An' Ma Tooley used to, when her husband's trawler came home. Grand times they were, too. This place would ring with good cheer.' It was silent now, except for the blackbirds in the garden, and the creak of floorboards as they moved from room to room.

Mrs McFee showed her into the main bedroom, which was tucked under the eaves. 'I'd like to a' lived here mysel'. But our place is home and has been for years.' She tried to catch Mrs Boofus's eye. 'You've been even longer in yours, haven't you, Elna?'

Mrs Boofus said nothing and turned away. There was a long pause while she stared out of the window at the back garden and the heather-capped hillside beyond, trying to compose herself. It was clear Mrs McFee wouldn't break the silence, so she had to say something. 'But I don't know for how much longer,' she said at last, with a catch in her voice.

Mrs McFee seemed to expect this. 'What's Grundy said?' she asked in a matter-of-fact way, for which Mrs Boofus was grateful.

'What can he say? It won't be him as makes the decision. It'll be the higher-ups, an' all they see is money.

Homeless we'll be, Flossie. Homeless within weeks, and Lon with no job an' all, less'n he finds old Gumnor again.' She was crying freely now. 'Where can we go? What shall we do? Where will we live?'

Mrs McFee put her arm across Mrs Boofus's quivering shoulders, and waited for the sobs to abate. 'Here, Elna. You can come and live here. You and Lon and Rarty. That's why I brought you to see it.'

Mrs Boofus turned sharply towards her, open-mouthed but speechless.

'It was always Ma Tooley's wish that someone live here if her son couldn't be found. She couldn't stand to think of it bare and rotting after she'd gone.' Mrs Boofus's eyes grew wider and wider. She grasped Mrs McFee by the hand and squeezed tightly, but still could find no words.

Mrs McFee smiled to comfort her and went on: 'Made me promise, she did, promise to find someone to live in it and love it as she had. I can think of none better'n you.'

Mrs Boofus embraced her, crying and laughing and talking in a rush, all at the same time. 'Flossie, I'm . . . I'm . . . I don't know what to say . . . Sorry . . . Thank you, oh thank you . . . It's beautiful . . . I'm sorry . . . How can we ever thank you enough?'

Mrs McFee stepped back from this torrent, still smiling. ''Tis Ma Tooley's in need of thanks, not I.' She offered Mrs Boofus her handkerchief. 'An', besides, there's your Lon and my lads out hunting Gumnor, as we stand here guddlin'. I 'opes they find her yet. Mayhap they don't . . . well, you and I'll be neighbours. Plenty o' ways to thank a neighbour. Plenty o' ways.' Mrs Boofus returned the handkerchief. Her eyes were dry now.

CHAPTER SEVEN
THE STORM

JEB TOOK THE COLLEEN AWAY FROM THE shore to clear the harbour wall, and throttled down. They'd been all round Gallican, but he was in no hurry to tie up. He muttered to Will, then called to the others on deck. 'I reckon we've time to circle Jetta too. What d'you say?' He was looking at Mr Boofus. Both of them knew that if they were to find Gumnor it would be on Gallican; searching Jetta was a way to put off admitting defeat.

Mr Boofus checked the sun. 'Aye,' he replied gruffly. 'There's time enough and more.' Jeb spun the wheel and the Colleen heeled to starboard as she turned away from the harbour into the fast-running tides of the strait.

Will dug some chunks of bread and cheese out of a haversack inside the wheelhouse and passed them round, together with a flask of hot, sweet tea. 'A bite, lass, while we cross to Jetta?' he asked Rarty, who was still intently scanning Gallican's fast-receding beaches. 'You won't see nothing from here, even with them glasses.'

Rarty unplugged the binoculars from her eyes just long enough to shake her head. 'No thank you,' she said. 'I'm really not hungry.'

Lionel was. It seemed ages since breakfast in the Boofus's cottage. He turned away from the rail, but his land-lubber's legs weren't ready for the way the deck was pitching now. He staggered forward, caught one foot on a coiled rope and sprawled full length, scattering lobster pots on to startled dogs, and upending the still-hot tea over Will's feet.

'Steady there, lad,' said Will as he picked Lionel up. When Lionel had gathered himself together, restacked the lobster pots and recovered his wits, Will took him by the shoulders and sat down in front of him. Lionel was frightened, and stammered an apology, but there was a kindly glint in Will's eyes. 'Don't look so afeared,' he said softly. 'That's warmed my feet up nicely. But always remember this first rule for a crewman at sea: one hand for the ship, one hand for yourself. Say it after me.'

Lionel faltered at first but, as he saw he was not about to be punished for his clumsiness, he grew in confidence and eventually, on his third attempt, he sang out loudly: 'ONE HAND FOR THE SHIP, ONE HAND FOR YOURSELF.'

There was a sudden silence and Lionel felt the stern eyes of John Quarrie, Mr Boofus and Jeb all bearing down upon him. What had he done wrong now?

Will was mortified. He went over to Mr Boofus. 'I'm terrible sorry,' he mumbled. 'I clean forgot. It just slipped out, like.' He fiddled with his marlin-spike. 'It's been so long, you see.'

Mr Boofus looked at him. 'Yes,' he said sadly. 'It's been so long I'd near forgot mysel'. Or I thought I had.' There was a pause. 'Does he talk at all?'

'Not a word,' said Will. 'He understands, all right, and he has ways of making us know he wants something. But he ain't spoke since the last time you saw him, and you know how long ago that was.'

Lionel understood none of this. Rarty was mystified too. 'Pa?' she asked. He didn't seem to notice. 'Pa?' she tried again, louder. This time he caught her eye, but didn't seem to know what to say.

John Quarrie broke in. 'I'll talk to 'er, Lon, if you like.'

Mr Boofus seemed relieved. 'Aye. Thank you, John. The lad too, I reckon. He'll know soon enough.'

John Quarrie took Lionel and Rarty by the hand and

led them up to the bows, where he sat them down on upturned fish crates between the two dogs, who had settled down to their dozing once more.

'The *Unicorn* she were called. Out in the Southern Ocean. Years ago now, before either o' you or either o' these 'ere dogs were born, your pa and Waldo and me, we sailed together in 'er. Best mates we were. Everywhere together – round the Horn, crossing the Line, storm or calm – never apart. Till the *Unicorn*, that was. A sweet vessel but old, you see. We should 'a run before the storm, not taken it on, but Cap'n Murphy allas were a stubborn man . . . Like the rest of us, I suppose. It weren't 'is fault – we were with 'im in 'is choice, but it were the wrong choice.

'Anyways, there we were, the three of us, up in the rigging, reefing the mains'l as the storm blew up. She were pitching and rolling but we were set for that. Years of practice, see – that and the golden rule: one 'and for the ship, one 'and for yourself.

'The storm hit hard and sudden, like, before we'd got all the sails in. We were struggling with the canvas when there were this terrible crash – I can almost 'ear it now – as the main mast snapped.' He paused, looking upwards. 'For an instant I thought it were thunder, but I knew, we all knew. There's no sound like it. We looked up to see the mast and spars and sails and rigging come crashing down towards us.'

Rarty was wide-eyed, imagining the terror. Her father had never told her any of this. She joined Lionel in watching John Quarrie intently as he went on. He seemed to be speaking to the wind or the birds or the sea, rather than to them.

'Nothing we could do. I were closest to the mast and I reached out to the ladder rigging. Something 'it me 'ere' – he lifted his cap to show a jagged scar on his left temple – 'and I were knocked out cold. I came round soon after, to a terrible sight. There was Waldo, obviously hurt bad, and there was your pa next to 'im. He was knocked about a bit, but he seemed all right. Both were tangled in the rigging, and the spar we'd all been on was almost sundered through. It were going to fall any moment and go crashing down on to the deck or into the water below. Either way the game were up.'

Rarty looked back to the afterdeck. Her father and Will were talking, but her father was casting glances up to the bows. He looked away when Rarty saw him. John Quarrie went on with his terrible tale. 'I tried to get up but I couldn't move. My leg were bust.' He patted his left knee. 'All I could do was watch. Such a sight. Your pa . . .' He faltered, looking down at Rarty, then cleared his throat and continued. 'Your pa . . . bravest thing I ever saw . . . Your pa, battered as he was, swinging about on a half-bust boom above a raging sea, 'e didn't come towards me, towards the mast, to save 'isself. No. He went back out. He went back for Waldo.

'The lads below, some of them, they were starting up the rigging to 'elp us, but it was all torn away. They watched as they struggled upwards; others watched while they worked on the deck; the 'elmsmen watched as they fought with the wheel. We all watched your pa.

'He got out to where Waldo was, all right, and freed 'im from the tangle and got 'im swung over 'is shoulders. Waldo was yelling to leave him, to save 'isself. He wouldn't. He started back, but what with the wind and the pitching of the ship and the battering 'e'd taken 'isself, he couldn't 'old Waldo *and* 'old on too. So what does 'e do, your pa? He forgets the golden rule, 'e does. One 'and for the ship, one 'and for hisself. Well, 'e needed both for Waldo. I saw 'im as he made up 'is mind what to do. If 'e let go, surely 'e'd be pitched off, Waldo and all. If 'e didn't, then 'e couldn't get Waldo back. And any moment the spar would break.'

John Quarrie shook his head. Rarty held her breath. 'He let go. I could barely watch. All the while Waldo's yelling at 'im, yelling in pain. And 'e let go. He locked his legs into such rigging as 'e could find, and 'e grit his teeth, and I think 'e mumbled a prayer, and 'e let go. He 'eld on with 'is legs, swinging and swaying and blowing about, and scrambling 'is way back, foot by foot, back to where I was, 'elpless at the mast. The strength it took. I knew 'e were a strong man – still is – but the strength it must 'a taken to do that, I don't know where 'e found it. Twice 'e nearly fell, but 'e wouldn't let go of Waldo, 'e wouldn't let 'im slip.

'At last 'e reached me. I grabbed 'old of Waldo. A pitiful sight 'e was, all mangled up and bloody. Some of the other lads 'ad clambered up to us, and they caught 'old of us three.' He stopped for a moment, looking back to the wheelhouse. His voice was different, softer somehow, when he spoke again. 'Together, even then, you see.

'It was then, when we knew we were safe, if broken and bruised, that the boom finally gave way and crashed into the sea below. Well, the lads got us down and into the sick bay. Out came the grog tub, for your pa and me. It eased the pain for us, but Waldo was past drinking it. Alive, yes, but only just.

'It took 'ours for the storm to abate, and the lads to secure what were left of the mast. By the time the surgeon came to set my leg and stitch up my 'ead 'ere, the grog tub was all but done, and I were right glad of it too. None of us thought poor Waldo would live till we reached port, but islanders are tough, and live 'e did. Trouble is . . . some thought better 'e 'adn't . . . and Waldo were one of them.'

Rarty caught Lionel's eye as John Quarrie continued. 'Bones can be set and bruises will fade and wounds will 'eal in time, but nothing and nobody could fix Waldo's back. Busted it was. All strength and feeling in 'is legs 'ad gone and gone for ever. If 'e were to move it had to be pushed about in a wheelchair like his old grandma. He 'ated it, 'ated every moment, after a life at sea on all the oceans of the world. And 'e came to 'ate it that your pa 'ad rescued 'im like 'e 'ad. He didn't 'ate your pa. Never that. But 'e hated it that your pa had saved 'im, only to leave 'im, as he saw, 'alf a man. He kept 'is 'ate of this to 'isself, till one day 'e could keep it no more. "Why?" 'e asked your pa. "Why did you do it? You knew the rule – one 'and for the ship, one 'and for yourself. But you broke it. You broke me. I'd rather you'd left me and I'd a' died, not while away my days like this. It's no life, no life for a man like me. I 'ate it. One 'and for the ship, one 'and for yourself!" He was terrible angry, raging and yelling, awful to behold.'

John Quarrie's eyes were glittering. He patted Port

gently on the head, and the dog repaid him by licking his hand. There was a long silence. Eventually he cleared his throat loudly and began to speak again. 'None of us ever went to sea again, not on a long voyage at least. I took the cottage on the beach where you found me not long past. Your pa, 'e started tending Gumnor and moved off the islands to your little place by the bridge. And Waldo . . . well 'e didn't say anything after 'is outburst at your pa for a day or so. Everyone waited for 'im to speak again . . . but 'e never did. No one can say why not. So the last words 'e uttered were the same as you sang out just now, lad. That's why they bothered us all so bad. They carry an 'eavy meaning, especially for your pa, and for me. An 'eavy, 'eavy meaning.'

John Quarrie fell silent. He seemed drained, exhausted. Lionel looked at him as he stared out to sea. Neither he nor Rarty knew what to say, and both were surprised and a little relieved when at length he spoke again.

'I think of this a lot,' he said, 'October days like these. It's getting towards winter and my old leg aches.' He rubbed it. 'It sets me to thinking. I've always thought the three of us would be together again. I didn't know when or 'ow. 'Tis a shame it should take the loss of Gumnor to make it 'appen. Still, there it is.'

He laid his left hand on Lionel's shoulder, his right

on Rarty's, and he looked at them for the first time in a long while. He didn't seem so far away any more. He bent down, smelling of fish, but not so strongly now, and smiled a crooked smile at each in turn. 'And if you 'elp us find Gumnor now, who knows what might 'appen next, eh?'

'Another log there, Lionel, if you would,' said Mrs McFee. Lionel left the table to collect another chunk of driftwood from the pile beside the fire. He liked this wood. It had been rubbed pebble-smooth in its journey to the shore, and smelt of salt and seaweed when it burnt. He liked the animal shapes it took. The last had been a giraffe, but he wasn't sure about this one.

Rarty didn't hesitate. 'Anteater,' she said. He didn't see it. 'Turn it over,' she suggested as he fumbled with it. 'No, the other way.' Suddenly it made sense, and he realised he *did* know what an anteater looked like after all.

'Anteater?' asked Mrs Boofus. 'What on earth's an anteater, then?'

Lionel turned to Rarty. He wasn't sure enough to try and describe it himself. Rarty took the wood and held it out in front of her. 'It's a shaggy thing with four legs and a tail, like Starboard but smaller. It's got a long pointy nose – here – with a tongue curled up inside, all sticky, to pick up the ants. That's all it eats.' Mrs Boofus screwed up her nose.

'It lives in the forest in Brazil or somewhere,' said Lionel.

'How do you two know all this?' asked Mrs McFee. 'I've never heard tell of such a thing.' She wondered if they were making it up.

'At school. Animals of the world,' said Rarty.

'She was top of the class, as usual,' said Lionel, torn between envy and pride.

'And what kind of job will you be fit for, knowing all about foreign snouty creatures what eat nothing but bugs, eh?' asked Mrs McFee, only partly in jest.

Rarty, suddenly deflated, was lost for words. She looked to Lionel for support, and he did not fail her. 'Anteater keeper,' he said firmly. 'Hours are bad – nocturnal, you know – but there's prospects. Keep its nose clean, five years on you move up to wombat. Wallaby even.'

There was a pause. One or two of the adults exchanged silent glances, then Rarty sniggered and the whole table, Lionel included, burst into laughter. Mrs McFee looked at him. 'What a strange boy you are,' she said. 'Wherever do you get such notions?'

Lionel's reply was stifled by an odd kind of snorting

noise from the head of the table. He looked up to see Waldo rocking backwards and forwards, spilling crumbs from his mouth and making strange harrumphing sounds.

Will jumped to his feet. 'Quick, Ma,' he said. 'He's got some food stuck again.'

Mrs McFee dashed round to stand behind her husband, and was just about to strike him firmly on the back, as she had on many previous occasions, when she stopped, arm raised, with an uncertain look on her face. Slowly, her puzzled concern gave way to wonder. 'No,' she said, in tones of quiet disbelief. 'Not food, Will. Not this time. Listen. He's laughing. *Laughing*, I tell you. Listen everyone.'

She sat down slowly and reached for her husband's hand where it lay by his plate. He was still snorting, although his rocking had slowed. She, her two sons and all their guests watched in fascination as, for the first time in many years, he took her hand clumsily in his. Rarty noticed that although he was not looking at anyone round him, his gaze was no longer fixed in the distance. He was *in* the room at last. She followed his stare, and realised he was looking at the anteater driftwood.

'I believe you're right, Ma. It *is* a laugh,' said Jeb in amazement. He looked at Lionel. 'An extraordinary thing you've done, lad. Truly extraordinary.'

The snorting died away and the rocking stopped. No more crumbs fell. 'Pa?' asked Jeb, but he was gone again, the horizon stare as hard as ever.

'Waldo?' asked his wife. 'Waldo?' He had let go her hand and was sitting iceberg-still once more. 'They reached you, didn't they, these young 'uns? Reached you where we couldn't, all these years. I've always known you were in there, Waldo. Always known it.' There were tears in her eyes. 'Please let us in again.'

Mrs Boofus, keen to give her hosts some privacy, stood up briskly. 'Come on, you two,' she said to Lionel and Rarty. 'We'll do the dishes. It's the least we can do after such a lovely meal. She bustled them off to the kitchen, calling over her shoulder to her husband, 'Lon, you bring the things through, will you?'

Even with the two of them drying, Rarty and Lionel could not keep up with Mrs Boofus's dishwashing speed. Soon the kitchen was piled high on all sides with steaming plates and saucepans. In an effort to slow her down, Rarty at last asked the question that had bothered her most of the evening. 'What will we do tomorrow, Ma? There's still a couple of days left to try and find Gumnor.' She knew in her heart that the day's fruitless trips round Gallican and Jetta were their last real chance, but she could not face the prospect of sitting around, waiting for Grundy's deadline to expire.

'There's not much we can do, love. You know that there won't be the boat? It's a slim living off the fish, and for Will and Jeb to leave off even for a day to help us, why, that were a big thing they did.' Her dishwashing had not slowed at all.

Rarty wiped another plate dry. 'But that means we're stuck on Gallican till the Monday ferry comes,' she protested, even though she wasn't sure where else she wanted to search.

'I know,' said her mother. 'We'll just have to make the best of it, that's all. There's nothing else to be done. Where else can we look that we've not picked over? We could search the world and still not find her.'

'Well, I'm not giving up like that,' said Rarty. She was getting angry.

Mrs Boofus tried to calm her. 'Why don't you come and look at Ma Tooley's place with me? There's a lovely little room you could have.'

'I'm not ready to leave the room I've got,' she said stubbornly. Mrs Boofus had never seen her like this. 'She's out there somewhere, I know it, and I mean to go on trying to find her until there's nowhere else to look.' Rarty flung down her tea-towel and returned to the front room for more dishes.

Mrs Boofus sighed and turned to Lionel. 'Can you make her see sense? Perhaps she'll listen to you.'

'I don't think so, Mrs Boofus,' he replied, shaking his head thoughtfully. 'She's very . . . headstrong.' He looked up with a wry smile. 'It's one reason why I like her.'

Mrs Boofus handed him a saucepan. 'If we do move over here,' she began with some hesitation. '*If*, you understand . . . you'll come and visit, won't you? Come as much as you like.'

He broke into a broad grin, whose warmth surprised her. 'I'd *love* to. I'd come whenever I could. Whenever they let me. This' – he swept his arm round, but Mrs Boofus wasn't sure if he meant the kitchen, or the McFees' cottage, or the hamlet by the harbour, or the whole of Gallican, perhaps even all the islands – 'this is such a . . . such a . . . *good* place.'

'A good place for what?' asked Mr Boofus, bringing a pile of plates into the kitchen. Rarty followed with more.

'We're talking about tomorrow, Lon,' said Mrs Boofus.

'Aye. I guessed, judging by the frown on yon lass's face.' He knew he had to come up with something to pacify Rarty. He also wanted to feel *he* was doing something, and it wouldn't be easy to sit in the cottage with Waldo all day. He looked out of the window towards the darkened harbour. Some of the boats carried

117

lights, doubled by their reflections into a quiet display of red, white and green. He stared for a long time, before abruptly turning back to the room. 'Why don't we all go up to Ma Tooley's place together and look it over? When we've done that, the youngsters can carry on up to Parson's Peak.' He spoke directly to Rarty now. 'You can near enough see the whole island from there. Ask Jeb if you can borrow his telescope, and you'll be able to survey all the beaches without having to tramp all over. If it's clear you can see offshore aways, too. No point us old folk going up. Our eyes will see nowt.'

Rarty had lost her angry scowl. 'Can we take the dogs, Ma?' she asked brightly.

'I'm sure they'll be glad of the walk. Best ask Mrs McFee though, eh, love?'

The room was dark, except for the driftwood embers glowing sunset red in the hearth. It was quiet too, apart from the whimpers of Port and Starboard chasing dream rabbits as they slept either side of the fire. Waldo sat in his wheelchair by the chart table, swaddled in blankets, as immobile as a ship's figurehead. Not much different when he's awake, thought Rarty.

'Are you asleep?' she whispered to the dark shape in the next hammock.

'Yes,' said Lionel.

A minute passed, then another, broken only by crackling from the fire. 'Stupid answer,' said Rarty. Sometimes Lionel did irritate her.

More time passed, and then he spoke: 'Silly question, really,' he muttered defensively. He'd have to try some more grown-up jokes. 'No, I'm not sleeping,' he said, to make up for it. 'I'm listening to the ship. I have to go on watch soon. It sounds very calm.'

It had felt like a ship since Rarty had asked where they were to sleep, earlier in the evening. Mrs McFee had pointed upwards.

'Upstairs?' Mrs Boofus had asked. 'Surely you don't have room?' Mrs McFee had indicated two sets of dull metal bars protruding from the ceiling beams, about eight feet apart.

'Not upstairs. Here.'

Rarty had understood immediately. 'Hammock bars!' she had cried. She was very excited. Although she'd secretly swung in the *Kraken*'s hammocks, she had never slept in one.

'You'll have to be quiet, mind,' Mrs McFee had said. 'Waldo sleeps down here in his chair. Can't lie down proper now, you see. So none of your chatter' – to Rarty – 'or your silliness,' – to Lionel. They had agreed eagerly.

Now, some hours later, Rarty was glad to find Lionel sharing her love for anything to do with the sea, and imagining, as she had, that they were below decks in some old sailing vessel. She followed his lead: 'Yes. I've just been on deck. It's a lovely night. The moon's out. There's flying fish.'

'And phosphorescence?' he asked.

'What?'

'Phosphorescence. You know, when things glow in the water, at night. The fish might. I've read about it but never seen it.'

'I know what you mean. I didn't know that was the word for it. I saw it sometimes from Pa's boat, when we went out to Gumnor in the dark. Like a kind of shimmer at the end of the oars. I thought it was something wrong with my eyes to begin with. Pa says it's ghost lights from wrecked ships and drowned sailors.'

'That makes it sound scary,' said Lionel. He hadn't imagined it that way.

'It's not,' said Rarty. She could almost see it now. 'It's beautiful, like liquid silver, but with blue in it. You want to put your hand in to catch it, but as soon as you do it's gone.'

'Evanescent, then.'

'You're showing off again. Everwhat?'

'Evanescent. Only there for a moment.' Lionel paused. 'As soon as you want it, it disappears. All the best things are like that.'

Rarty thought about this for a while. 'No they're not,' she said.

'Yes they are.'

Louder now: 'No they're *not*.' Their talking woke Starboard. They watched in silence as he got up, looked sleepily about him, turned a complete circle and flopped heavily down again, with a loud sigh. He was back to sleep in seconds.

'Yes they are,' whispered Lionel. 'Name one good thing that isn't.'

Rarty thought hard. She was sure he was wrong. 'The surf at Point Rey,' she said. 'It's always there, pounding away. Or the golden rocks at Bollings. They've been there for millions of years. They're good things, not evan – evan – whatever you said.'

'Yes, they're good things,' Lionel conceded. 'But they change all the time. The surf – every wave is different. You can never stop one and hold it.'

'What about the rocks, then?' Surely she had him now.

'They change too. I watched them all day once. In the morning, with the sun behind them, they're grey. In the middle of the day they're nearly white. When the sun is going down, they glow red and gold and orange, even purple, and they're changing all the time. You can take a picture but you know they won't be the same when you come back.'

Rarty thought harder, swinging gently in her hammock. He was twisting things. 'Gumnor,' she said at length. 'She didn't change. She was always there, the same. She'll be the same now, wherever she is.'

Lionel had no reply.

'I still hope we'll find her.' Rarty was talking to herself now, as much as to him. 'Then you'll see. She's one of the best things. She's *the* best thing.'

There was a long silence. A driftwood log settled in the hearth, raising some sparks and a short-lived flickering flame. Something – two things – over beside the chart table glittered in this brief light. Rarty was trying to make out what it was when Waldo began to splutter. The dogs raised their heads to look on as he stirred in his chair. Had he been awake, listening to them? Had they woken him up? There would be trouble from Mrs McFee for this.

Waldo *was* awake. He kept making the same noise again and again, something between a hiss and a rattle. It didn't make any kind of sense.

Rarty and Lionel looked at each other. They didn't

know what to do. The dogs were standing now, either side of Waldo's chair, looking at him uneasily as the hissing continued. This must be unusual for them too, thought Rarty. They looked so worried.

'We'd better see to him,' she said, clambering down gingerly from her hammock. She crept over towards Waldo. In the dim red glow she could see that his eyes – two glittering things – were fixed on the chart table in front of him. His hissing grew louder as she approached. Rarty listened hard, trying to make sense of it.

There was a sudden clatter and thump, followed by a muffled 'Ouch!' in the corner behind her. Lionel joined her, rubbing his elbow and wincing.

She looked at him. 'You're so clumsy.'

'Sorry,' said Lionel. No one had told him there was a knack to getting out of a hammock. 'Look,' he pointed as Waldo's right hand emerged from beneath his blankets, like a wary eel from its lair. With an obvious effort and painful slowness, he stretched his hand across the table and stabbed his forefinger awkwardly down. His hissing was louder still.

They nudged the dogs aside to bend over the table. 'It's a map of Gallican,' said Lionel. 'But where's he pointing?' They struggled to make it out, but Waldo's finger was trembling so much it covered most of Gallican and parts of Jetta too. He couldn't keep it still, and the harder he tried to control it, the worse things became.

'Wait a minute,' said Lionel. 'What's he saying?'

'It's just a noise,' said Rarty. 'A noise to wake us up.'

'No, he's saying something.' He bent to speak into Waldo's ear. 'You're trying to tell us something, Mr Waldo, aren't you?' There was no response. Lionel straightened up. 'It sounds like . . . sounds like . . .' A dim but recent memory floated towards the surface of his mind. 'I know it, I'm sure. It sounds like . . . when you walk on sand . . . you told me . . . there's a word. An islander word.'

'Scrasser,' said Rarty.

'Yes, yes, that's it. That's the one.' They both looked at Waldo. His finger was still spidering all over Gallican, but his hissing had stopped.

'It is scrasser, Mr Waldo, yes?' Lionel was excited. 'A beach, that's what you're telling us. But which one? There's so many, and we went all round them. We looked and looked. She wasn't there. *Which* scrasser, Mr Waldo? Which one?'

Slowly Waldo's finger grew still. His hand withdrew inside his blankets and he sat back in his chair, exhausted. He made no further sound, and sat motionless once more, except for his mouth. His lips were moving silently, making the same shapes again and again. They watched him intently, trying to understand, but he grew more and more tired, and his mouthings grew vaguer, until finally they stopped and he fell asleep once more.

Rarty was distraught. 'What now? He's trying to tell us she's on a beach somewhere. We know that. Where else would she be but on a beach, washed up like some old dead fish? We need to know *which* beach. And how does he know, anyway? It's no good.'

'Remember how he knew we were coming today?' said Lionel. 'I think maybe he knows lots of things.' He drew her away. 'Come on, Rarty. We mustn't bother him any more or we'll be in trouble.'

The dogs had already returned to the hearth, and they stepped over them to get to the hammocks. 'Help me in,' said Lionel. Rarty obliged, then swung smoothly into her own hammock.

They lay there, lost in their own thoughts. Lionel listened to Rarty's breathing change as she fell asleep, then began to practise Waldo's mouth movements over and over, varying them slightly to see what noises might come out. There had been a word there. He would find it. He would.

CHAPTER EIGHT
THE CALL

'SOME MORE PORRIDGE, LASS?' ASKED MRS McFee. She was trying to catch Rarty's eye. 'A long morning ahead, and none too warm.'

'I will please, Mrs McFee, yes,' said Rarty.

'Here then, love. Pass us your bowl.' Rarty looked up as she did so. Mrs McFee had her eye at last. 'Now you're *sure* you didn't trouble Waldo last night? Rare difficult to wake he was.'

Rarty shook her head, and looked away. 'Maybe he's just tired having us all around,' she said. At least she wasn't lying outright.

'Maybe so,' said Mrs McFee. She was still suspicious – Waldo hadn't been *that* tired – but she let Rarty finish her porridge in peace.

Breakfast was followed by a great putting-on of coats

and gloves and jumpers. Mrs McFee tucked a rug over Waldo's legs as he dozed, and they set off: six people, two dogs, and a wheelbarrow laden with tools and wood and curtains, trundling up the hill to Ma Tooley's cottage, their breath-clouds merging with each other and the fog around them.

Lionel and Rarty hung back, mainly to avoid further questions from Mrs McFee, but also because Rarty was still hobbled and sore from her cuts and bruises.

Lionel taunted her about this. 'How's the rheumatics, Grandma?' he asked, shuffling alongside her, stooped and mock-weary, but careful to keep out of range. 'Life, eh? Fair wears you out, it does,' he sighed.

The *Colleen*'s deck felt oddly empty, lacking dogs and visitors, but Will knew that if the day went well it would soon be alive with silvery glittering fish, spilled from the nets they had just set. Somehow, though, there never seemed to be as many as he recalled from his boyhood, and those they did catch were a little smaller every year.

'Listen,' called Jeb from the bows. Will couldn't hear anything, so he left the wheelhouse to join him. Everything was still and grey, the fog muffling all sounds into a soft and woolly hush. Will shook his head. 'I can't hear anything,' he said. 'What was it?'

Jeb frowned, beginning to doubt himself. 'I'm not sure. I thought at first a foghorn, but it didn't make sense.' They were miles offshore, and far from any shipping lanes.

Will peered into the fog. He could see no more than the vessel's length ahead. If there was a ship, perhaps off course, bearing down on them, there would be no warning, just its looming bulk above and then the splintering of wood. He shivered at the thought. 'I'll cut the engine,' he said.

Without the engine's heartbeat throb, the silence was total now. Neither wished to break it by breathing.

'There,' said Jeb.

Will had heard it too: a low and long-drawn mournful monotone away off to starboard. 'Any closer?' he asked.

Jeb shook his head. 'Don't think so. Moving east, I'd say.'

'A ship, then,' said Will. 'We'd best let 'em know we're here.' He turned towards the wheelhouse to restart the engine and sound the siren, but was stopped in his tracks by another sound, identical to the first, but this time off to port.

He and Jeb looked at each other. They didn't understand. 'Start her up or no?' asked Will. Jeb shrugged. Neither knew what to do.

The starboard sound repeated again, but differently, with a shorter, deeper note below the first. 'There's two there now,' Jeb said, perplexed. 'This ain't ships, Will.'

'What then?' asked Will. A further call came, this time astern, to be answered by another, off the port bow. The *Colleen* was surrounded. More calls came, faster and louder, from all directions. Before long the individual sounds merged into one, with no breaks between. The chorus swelled to fill the air and sea all around, and the hull of the *Colleen* hummed in resonance.

Will felt a lump in his throat. Whatever made this noise, it was beautiful. The plaintive, haunting tones filled him with a nameless ancient yearning, which he felt in his blood but could not understand. Jeb had sensed it too. Will could see his eyes shine as he looked about him, stunned in wonder.

Still the sound rose, until it seemed it could get no louder. It was no longer possible to tell where the noise began and ended. They and their vessel were becalmed amid an invisible choir singing a song which ached with sadness. They were *in* the sound, almost part of it. Then, at the very peak, a new sound was added: the rippling of water, close by.

'Look!' cried Jeb.

A dark shape broke the slate-smooth water alongside and then was gone, calling loudly as it vanished in the fog. Two more, one large and one small, followed, the smaller giving a higher, weaker call as it passed. One after another, dim underwater figures swept past the boat on both sides, just breaking the surface with their backs, and leaving a silvery wake behind.

'Creatures,' said Will. 'Scores of them.' He felt a bump, but no fear, as one of them brushed against the *Colleen*. He knew they were safe from these gentle visitors.

'Creatures, all right,' said Jeb. 'But what kind? I've never seen nor heard such as these.' The sound began to die away, like a fast-ebbing tide. A monstrous barnacled back swept by and ended the chorus with a massive final blast, to leave a ringing silence. The sea resumed its glassy smoothness as this, the last of the great beasts, disappeared into the fog ahead.

'Nor I,' replied Will. But there *was* something familiar about them. 'Leastways not at sea, not like this.'

The same thought occurred to them both at the same time. 'You mean –' Jeb began.

'Yes,' Will replied. 'That call, those backs. Just like old Gumnor, I'd say.'

'But I thought she were the last.'

'Aye, so did we all. It seems she ain't.' Will paused, staring after them. 'I reckon we've just seen something rare, Jeb, something fine.'

Jeb nodded. 'A privilege, it is. And not just what we've seen. That sound. I'll never forget it.' He too was gazing into the fog. The sound had gone and the water was still. Already it was almost as if it had never happened. 'East of here is . . .'

'Gallican. We'd best get back.'

'And this would be your room,' said Mrs Boofus, opening the door to a little L-shaped attic bedroom. Even without curtains or furniture it felt cosy, but Rarty did no more than glance inside.

'Don't you want to look round?' asked her mother, exasperated.

'No, Ma.' Rarty wouldn't consider moving out of her old room where she had lived all her life until she was sure that Gumnor was gone.

Her mother persisted. 'It will look lovely, with all your things here. They'll fit just right. We can crochet a new bedspread, all bright like. I can picture it.'

Somehow Rarty found the strength to go against her mother for the first time. She knew it would hurt. 'I'm not going in, Ma. Please don't ask me again. I just won't.'

Mrs Boofus stood in the doorway, too upset to speak, looking to her husband. There was an uneasy pause, broken by a hammering below.

'That's Mr Quarrie starting on the windows, Rarty. He'll need a hand fetching timber and such,' Mr Boofus said. 'We'll set to up here with the curtains. When you're done you can go on up to Parson's Peak.'

'Even with the fog?' asked Rarty. She had assumed it would be pointless.

'Aye. I think it'll clear afore noon,' replied her father. He knew it wouldn't. The fog was set to last all day and more, but he wanted to give Rarty some hope to hang on to. 'Only you're to go no further, mind. I'll be blowed if I'll tramp over these hills after you and the lad here if'n you gets lost.'

Rarty rushed off downstairs, dragging Lionel behind her. Mr Boofus called after them. 'And if the fog don't lift, you're to come right back, lass.' She shouted her agreement from the bottom of the stairs.

'You know some islander, Rarty,' said Lionel. He was picking through the wood in the wheelbarrow. 'Is there a word that sounds like . . . something like "clundiss"?'

Rarty shook her head. 'Not that I know. But I don't know that much.' She took the piece of wood he

132

handed her, and balanced it on top of the others in her arms. 'Why?'

'It could be "clundish" or "clundiff" even. Something like that. I'm not sure.'

'I still don't know any. And you haven't told me why you want to know.' She was thinking about the way she had refused her mother, and Lionel's questions were an irritating distraction.

'Waldo, last night. He called the beach a scrasser. He was speaking islander. The other word –'

Rarty cut him short. 'It wasn't a word. Just noise. Don't talk about this. You know what'll happen if they find out we woke him up.' Her voice had dropped to an angry hiss and her eyes kept flicking upwards to the room above them where her parents were working on the curtains. 'I've upset Ma enough already.'

Lionel saw her anger but wouldn't give up. 'You only think it wasn't a word because it was a word you don't know,' he whispered. 'It was islander. It means something, I'm sure.' Rarty lost her patience and turned for the door, to be passed on the threshold by John Quarrie, who had come out to see what was keeping them.

Lionel didn't see him, for he was bent over the barrow, rummaging among the timber for the pieces he had been sent to fetch. 'Clundiss . . . clundiff . . .

clundish,' he muttered, bending over. 'Clundy . . . clundy . . . clundy.'

'That's right, lad.' Lionel was startled by John Quarrie's sudden deep tones behind him. 'But how did you know?'

Lionel straightened up, frowning. 'How did I know what?'

'The stuff you're holding there. The old islanders, they call it "clundy". Timber, you know, wood, lumber. I haven't heard the word for years. How come you know it?'

'I don't really,' replied Lionel, trying to suppress his rising excitement. He was close now, very close. 'I must have read it in a book at home.' He paused. 'Is there . . . is there a word like it, a longer one, like clundiff or clundiss?'

John Quarrie scratched his head. 'I'm . . . I'm not sure,' he said slowly. 'It's been a long time.' The wheels of his aging memory creaked into action.

Lionel was frantic. How long could he take? Did he know the word or not? Come on, thought Lionel. Come *on*.

At last John Quarrie's face brightened. 'Wait,' he said. (I *am* waiting, thought Lionel, jigging from foot to foot.) 'Wait. Yes. Yes, there is such a word. "Clundiff". It means something like a wooden wall, a fence.'

Lionel felt a sudden calm. 'You mean like a barricade?'

'Exactly so,' said John Quarrie. He was surprised and proud that his memory had not let him down. It was so rarely tested these days.

'Now, where's that other piece of two-by-four, lad?' he asked, turning to the barrow. 'You can be sure it'll be at the bottom, eh?' He glanced behind him. Lionel had vanished.

Rarty wrestled her hand free from Lionel's grip and stopped running. 'You've *got* to tell me what's going on,' she demanded breathlessly.

Lionel looked anxiously over her shoulder and, behind it, the hedge. He could still see the upper windows of the cottage, which meant Rarty's parents could see him, if they chose to look. 'Not here,' he said. He turned to face uphill. A little further up the track was a large chestnut tree, with a wide and deeply grooved trunk. They could stop there for a while. He pointed. 'At that tree.'

Rarty didn't move. 'What about these two?' she asked, patting Port on the head. The dogs had been chewing a bone each by the back door of the cottage when Lionel burst out and ran for the garden gate, dragging Rarty behind. Thinking this a game, they had followed, but were now as confused as Rarty, and were looking to her for guidance. 'We can't just disappear with their dogs.'

Lionel said nothing. He looked over the hedge again and set off uphill once more, this time at a fast walk rather than a run. 'The tree,' he said, over his shoulder. 'We'll talk there.'

Rarty stared after him, angry that there was no alternative but to follow. 'Come on, boys,' she muttered at length, biting her lip and setting off uphill.

When she reached the tree she found Lionel crouched low in the hollow of the trunk. She hunkered down beside him, but the dogs were still unsure. 'Come,' she said. 'Come on, Port. Come, Starboard.' They obeyed at once. 'Good boys. Now, sit.' They sat. 'That's it. Good boys. And *down*.' They settled, either side of the entrance to the hollow, their eyes fixed upon her, trusting and watchful. *Dogs are so much happier when you tell them what to do*, she thought. *Why isn't it like that for people?*

Lionel seemed in no hurry to explain. She turned to him. 'Well?' she demanded.

'I know where she is,' he said with a quiet confidence unusual for him. 'Gumnor,' he continued. 'I know where she is. Waldo *did* tell us last night –'

Rarty snorted with derision. 'Not that again,' she said.

Lionel raised his hand. 'Let me finish,' he said, with a firmness that silenced her. 'Just listen for a minute, that's all.' He paused to smile at Starboard, who was looking from one to the other as if he understood. 'Waldo, last night, what he said. I've worked it out. "Clundiff scrasser". That other word, it's "clundiff". John Quarrie told me what it means: barricade.' He turned to look at her. 'Don't you see? Clundiff scrasser . . . barricade beach . . . It's Logger's Strand – that beach where all the trees are piled up. *That's* what Waldo was trying to tell us. That's where she is.'

She looked steadily at him. 'But we went there yesterday – no sign of her. And what makes you think old Waldo would know anyway? All he does is sit inside all the time and –'

'Watch things. He watches things with his telescope, all day long. He might not talk, but he can still see what happens.'

Still Rarty resisted. Maybe he had something; maybe he was just being Lionel. 'Waldo can't see the other side of Gallican,' she said. She made it sound like the dark side of the moon.

Lionel was not easily dissuaded. 'Look. I *know* that's

where she is. We can go there now and find out for sure. It's not too far.' He looked at her, but she wouldn't meet his eye, preferring instead to fiddle with some of the many conkers that were scattered nearby, half emerged from their split pulpy shells.

He persisted. 'What are you going to do instead? Wait here, in the fog? Go home?' Rarty threw the conkers harder and harder against the ground, to break them free of their pods. Lionel paused, then played his trump card. 'Or are you going to help them hang up the curtains in your new room?'

Rarty turned to face him, her eyes hard and shiny. She hurled her last conker against the beech trunk opposite. The soft green-white husk spattered about, and the shiny brown nut bounced back hard enough to catch Port on his right flank. He yelped in pained surprise, then stretched to sniff with suspicion the still-spinning nut as it settled in the leaf-litter beside him. 'All right,' she said. 'All *right*. We'll go.' She had to take over now. 'With these two and the map we should find the way there and back easily enough.'

'Map?' asked Lionel, suddenly uncertain. 'Map?'

Rarty sensed an opportunity to even things up. 'Yes, Lionel, the map. Waldo's Gallican map. You were to bring it, remember?'

Lionel fumbled in his pockets, but he knew it wouldn't be there. He could see that Rarty knew it too, and gave up the pretence. 'I'll go and fetch it,' he said simply, getting to his feet.

'Yes,' said Rarty. 'You do that. I'll wait here.' She was in control again.

John Quarrie clomped upstairs. 'That's ground floor winders done,' he called to the empty landing. 'Any more up here?'

Mrs McFee's head popped round the bathroom door. 'Not in here, John. The main bedroom, though, you'll find one there.'

Mr and Mrs Boofus were busy hanging curtains inside. 'What do you think?' asked Mrs Boofus. Already she thought of the cottage as her new home.

John Quarrie looked about. He could tell from Mr Boofus's expression he shouldn't say too much. 'Lovely it is, Elna, really lovely.' He put down his tools. 'You've a window in here needs fixing?'

Mrs Boofus pointed to a broken pane in the smaller of the two windows. John Quarrie set to work. 'I'm just boarding them up for now, for warmth and dryness like,' he said. 'Glazing can come later . . . if needs still be.'

'The youngsters not with you then?' asked Mr Boofus as he stood there, enshrouded in curtain. 'I sent them down to help.'

John Quarrie laughed. 'Aye, and help they did, what with bringing the wrong wood in and clucking on about some old islander talk, and then, the moment I turn my back, they vanish. Left me talking to thin air like I were mad.' He measured up a piece of wood against the broken pane. 'I thought they'd shot off to play in the garden with the dogs.'

Mrs Boofus peered through the window. 'Funny. I've not seen them out there at all. Nor heard them neither. And not a peep from the dogs.' She turned to her husband. 'They wouldn't just vanish off to Parson's Peak without a word, would they, Lon?'

Mr Boofus sighed. 'The Lord alone knows, Elna. Young Rarty's in a funny mood this morning – you know that. They'll come to no harm, though. Yon dogs will see to that. Better off out of our hair for a while anyhow.'

His wife was not convinced, but returned to her curtain hanging. 'I don't know,' she muttered. 'I reckon they're up to something.'

Lionel crawled on all fours below the McFees' front hedge and stopped opposite the porthole window. He pulled off some twigs of privet and held them in front of his face, like a greenleaf fan, as he slowly got to his feet. He could see the glint of Waldo's spyglass through the privet screen, and the lumpy shape of Waldo, a-doze within.

He dropped the privet, undid the garden gate, and stole up to the front door. Taking a deep breath, he turned the door knob. He guessed that in a ship-shape dwelling like this the door-lock and hinges would be well-oiled and noiseless – and he was right – but he did worry about creaking floorboards.

He stood in the doorway, taking in the silence, which was broken only by the slow and solid ticking of a grandfather clock, and the uneven rasp of Waldo's breathing. *Definitely asleep*, thought Lionel, as he crept forward, testing each floorboard for creaks, like a mouse sneaking up on some cheese. At last he reached the chart table. Standing before it, with Waldo close enough to touch, he could see that the map of Gallican was laid out just as it had been the night before. All he had to do was to roll it up and retrace his steps. No one would ever know. He bent forward and slid the map towards him. Waldo didn't stir. *I wonder if he dreams?* thought Lionel. *I hope so. All those years . . . and not even dreaming.*

He peered closely at the map, tracing his finger over

the coastline. He could read all the markings now. Yesterday's boat trip had left him with no clear memory of how the different parts of the shore all fitted together, but he did remember Logger's Strand being bigger than the other beaches. His finger came to a halt on the biggest beach. 'Logger's Strand' was picked out in large black letters, but there was something else beneath it, in smaller, fainter type.

He slipped round a corner of the table to get a closer look. 'If this says what I think,' he said to himself, 'she'll *have* to believe me.' If he bent low and shaded the light from the window he could just make it out. 'Clundiff scrasser,' he whispered, smiling to himself. 'I knew it.'

He straightened up and slid the map slowly off the table, rolling it up as he did so. He winced every time the cloth-backed paper crumpled. How could paper make so much noise? At last he was done, and he turned from the table, clutching the tightly rolled map in both hands. Just as he began to relax, thinking himself safe, a bony hand clamped itself onto his shoulder.

'HOOOO!' said a breathy voice in his ear, as the talons bit through his jumper.

Lionel shrieked, a terrified mouse-boy, and scampered for the door, fearing behind him a vision from his dreams

— a monstrous owl swooping down, the cruel hook of its beak agape and hungry.

Lionel had to get outside to safety, for this was an indoor owl. His dash for the door broke the talons' grasp and triggered a noise, halfway between a cough and a splutter. It was familiar, but he didn't pause to identify it. He just ran. He hurtled through the door, stumbled over a lobster pot in the garden, cleared the garden gate in a single bound, and galloped up the hill, before collapsing to his knees on the verge, breathless, quivery and twitching.

A harsh cackle drifted up from the cottage far below. Lionel shivered. 'At least I've got the map,' he gasped, each raw breath hurting his throat. Slowly, his terror subsided, his breathing eased, and the tremor in his limbs came under control. He tried to separate in his mind the reality of what had happened from his imaginings and the dim memory of old nightmares. As the fear eased, he began to see the funny side of Waldo's prank, and he felt forced to admit it was just the sort of thing he'd do himself, given the chance.

Eventually, feeling more composed, he got to his feet, and headed on uphill, brushing the dust off his trousers and looking for something in the verge. He had an idea.

A pile of shiny conkers lay at Rarty's feet. She was polishing another when she spotted Lionel.

'What on earth . . . ?' she said, astonished at his bizarre appearance. A piece of rope was tied to his belt, and trailed along the ground behind him. His upper lip curled upwards, exposing his teeth, and holding in place, underneath his nose, some grass stalks. His arms were tucked up to his chest and his hands hung down, clutching the rolled-up map between them. He walked in an odd, scittery gait.

Rarty couldn't help herself. Any remaining irritation she felt for Lionel vanished in her stifled giggles. She called out to him in a passable imitation of John Quarrie, 'Come along now, lad. What are you, a man or a mouse?'

'Mouse,' squeaked Lionel. It was difficult to talk and keep the grassy whiskers in place. 'Most definitely mouse.' He handed her the map as she got to her feet. 'But I brought you the cheese. Snatched from the very beak of Owldo McFierce, raptor king, deep within his lair.'

Rarty took the map, but kept it rolled. 'Come on then, Mighty Mouse. Off we go.'

Lionel let the whiskers drop. 'Aren't you going to look at it?' he asked in his normal voice.

'At what?'

'The map I've just risked my tail for, that's what.' He wanted her to see he was right about the beach.

'Not here. Up at the top – it'll make more sense there.' She started uphill.

Lionel was dismayed. He hadn't wanted to gloat, but here he was, following in her wake, as she took charge again. The dogs looked up at him. 'I know,' he said to Port, with a sigh. 'You can't win.' He shrugged his shoulders, and set off in Rarty's footsteps, followed in turn by Port and Starboard, both fascinated by the new hempen tail he dragged through the grass behind him.

John Quarrie put down his hammer. 'That's us then, is it?' he asked.

'Aye,' said Mr Boofus. 'No more we can do just now. Elna won't see it so – she wants to move in tomorrow – but I think this watch is done. Let's go below.'

They clomped downstairs to join the women in the front room. 'Youngsters back yet?' asked John Quarrie.

Mrs Boofus shook her head, frowning. 'Not a peep,' she replied, then to her husband, 'I don't like the way she just takes off, Lon. She mustn't keep worrying us so.'

Mr Boofus looked at his watch. 'Well, it's lunch-time now. A good mornin's work all round. How say you we break off for a bite? Me and John here' – glancing at his old sea-mate – 'we'll head on up to the Peak and roust them down.' John Quarrie nodded his agreement. Mrs Boofus looked relieved. Her husband continued: 'Meet you both directly, back at yours, Flossie?'

'Sounds fine to me,' said Mrs McFee. 'I've a big pot o' broth a-warmin' in the hearth.' John Quarrie beamed. He hadn't eaten so well for years.

'Listen,' said Lionel. They were in an ancient wood on the far side of Parson's Peak. There was no path or track and Rarty, who had assumed the role of navigator, was concentrating on their route. It would be easy to get lost here.

'I can't hear anything,' she called over her shoulder as she walked on ahead. There was little undergrowth, the floor being a springy bed of pine needles, but there were lots of dead branches which cracked loudly when trodden on.

'I'm not surprised,' said Lionel. 'Just stop a moment and listen, will you, moosefeet. Crashing about like an overfed elk.'

That brought her to a halt. Lionel and the dogs stopped too. There was a pause, while Rarty at least pretended to listen. 'I still can't hear anything,' she said.

'Exactly.'

Rarty sighed. 'Lionel, we don't have time for any of your –'

'The silence. When was the last time you really heard silence?' He spread his arms wide and looked about him. 'Can you hear it now?'

Rarty listened again, this time properly. There was not a breath of wind to stir the leaves, and they were still too far from the beach for the surf sounds to carry. No birds were singing, no insects buzzed, no animals rustled nearby. Everything was still.

When Lionel spoke again, his voice seemed suddenly loud. He dropped it to a near-whisper. 'Where I live, there's always cars and buses and people and noise. It's never really quiet, even in the middle of the night. It's never like this.'

Rarty said nothing, though it occurred to her it was never really quiet where she lived either. The noise of the sea formed an ever-present background to her life. It was only now, when it wasn't there, that she fully realised this. She missed it, but Lionel was right – this woodland silence was special. She was glad to immerse herself in it with him, and slowly raised her arms too.

They stood enchanted, side by side, looking upwards, as if the only sound that could break the spell had to come from above. The dogs sat softly at their feet, their noses high in the air. Faint clouds of breath enshrouded the four of them, merging with the licks of fog that hung between the trees. It seemed to Lionel that if he stayed still just a little longer, arms aloft, motionless, hardly breathing, to drink in this silence, he would surely start to become a tree. The mosses and lichens, which covered the birch boles nearby, would appear on him as well. He checked his legs, in case they had already begun.

Looking up again, he caught a small movement in the branches overhead. A beech leaf, all copper and gold, was spinning slowly down. It drifted this way and that in the breathless air, brushing lightly against other, still-green, leaves in its leisurely descent.

'Catch it,' said Rarty. 'It's lucky if you catch them.'

Lionel cupped his hands together and fixed his eyes on the leaf as it drifted towards him. To catch it looked like it would be easy, too easy, as if any luck it brought would not amount to much – an extra sausage tonight, perhaps, or beating Rarty's pa at cards again. I want some big luck, thought Lionel, stretching his hands out in front of him. Let's see if it can catch me. He closed his eyes.

Rarty saw this. As the leaf descended between them she stretched silently to grasp it above her head. She placed it gently on Lionel's waiting palms. He opened his eyes to find her smiling at him. The leaf lay in his hands, fragile and luminous. He couldn't tell if it had settled there itself, or she had guided it down, and he didn't know what size luck it was if she had; but he returned her steady gaze, smiling back at her.

The spell was abruptly broken. A squirrel, whose unseen movements must have dislodged the leaf, descended as close as it dared and chittered angrily at the intruders. The dogs barked wildly, and ran in frantic circles, looking for any way to reach it.

The moment of peace and stillness had gone, and Lionel knew it. So did Rarty. 'We'd best move on,' she said. Her voice was softer than before.

Lionel agreed, slipped the leaf into the breast pocket of his shirt and set off again downhill, this time beside her.

'Come on, boys,' she called to the dogs, who reluctantly followed on, casting occasional glances over their shoulders. The squirrel's continued taunts slowly faded as they dropped down towards the beach.

Neither spoke for a while. Lionel thought about the leaf and the silence, as if by reliving the moment quickly now, while it was still fresh, he could somehow fix the magic in his memory. He was startled when, at length, Rarty spoke, and what she said surprised him even more.

'I was a birch,' she said. 'What were you?'

CHAPTER NINE
BEACHED

MR BOOFUS ROLLED THE CONKERS ROUND with his foot. 'I don't know what to make of this at all,' he said. 'They must have sat here a good time to shell all these spolders.' Already, after just two days back on the islands, he was using islander words more and more. 'But I thought they were keen as mustard to top the Peak. An' what this straw's all about beats me.'

'Onward and upward, Lon,' said John Quarrie. He was hungry for his lunch. 'I dursay they can tell us when we finds 'em.'

The two old sailors set off uphill. Mr Boofus noticed John Quarrie's limp. 'How is that leg o' your'n, then?' he asked.

'It stiffens, come the winter. Not sore exactly, but every year it needs more trampin' about the shingle to loosen in the morning.'

'That shore-front life you lead looks hard, John. How goes it for you?'

When eventually it came, John Quarrie's reply was gruff. 'Hard it is, and even if I weren't slowing down, it'd be harder each year. There's the seaman's pension, but you know what little that's worth. Barely keeps me in coal. Used to be driftwood a-plenty for burnin', but it's all this plastic now. Ugly stuff, awful to burn. Council give me pennies to gather what I can. They call it recyclin', or so – as if using summat more'n once were a new idea.' He grunted. 'There's a few lobster and crab still, but never enough to sell, and as for clothes – well I patch and mend as best I can. It's more darn than yarn on some.' He looked at Mr Boofus. 'My head's above water, Lon, but only just, and if my health goes I'm sunk. It'll be the Seaman's Rest for me.'

Mr Boofus began to wish he hadn't raised the question, but their arrival at Parson's Peak effectively changed the subject for him. The track ran out here, just below the summit, which was marked by a small stone cairn. On a good day the whole of Gallican's shoreline was clearly visible, but now the hilltop floated in a sea of fog, an island within an island; and Rarty, Lionel and the dogs were nowhere to be seen.

The two of them called and whistled, but there was no response. Mr Boofus was growing angry. 'You heard me tell 'em, John, did you not?'

'I did that,' replied John Quarrie, between loud whistles.

'You an' I have tramped after 'em enough these last few days. We're too old for this lark.' But both knew they'd do it again, and they set off down the far slope, Mr Boofus still grumbling away.

'That's odd,' said Mrs McFee. She and Mrs Boofus had nearly reached her cottage. She stopped and pointed towards the harbour. 'I'm sure that's the *Colleen* – but the lads weren't due back till dusk. I hope there's nothing wrong.'

As they entered the garden gate they could see that Waldo was not in his usual spot by the window. This again was odd. Drawing up to the door, they heard the sound of voices from within. Three voices. It didn't make sense.

Mrs McFee opened the door and stepped inside. There, by the fire, her two sons either side of him, sat her husband, engaged in some elaborate pantomime.

Waldo sat forward with his arms tucked under his chin. He wrinkled his nose and squeaked in a thin high-pitched voice, 'Lionel . . . eek . . . eek.' Will laughed, and

Waldo abruptly switched roles to sit immobile in his chair, his wide-eyed stare unblinking. He mimicked vigorously the rest of his prank – the silent unfurling of his bony arms, the loud and sudden 'HOOOOOOO!', the fingernails digging into Lionel's shoulder and its result: Lionel's terrified squeal and scuttle to safety. When the performance was done he sat back in his chair, laughing long and loud, till the tears came. Will and Jeb were laughing too. None of them had noticed the women by the door.

Mrs McFee was aghast. It seemed that after all these years her Waldo was still and silent no more, but his new-found voice and vigour only revealed a fate far worse: he had clearly gone mad. And here were her sons, home early to humour him in his dotage. She shifted from foot to foot, uncertain whether to interrupt or continue watching. A creaking floorboard made the decision for her. The laughter stopped abruptly, and three faces turned towards her.

After an awkward silence Will spoke up. 'It's all right, Ma,' he said, in an attempt to soothe her. 'It's a joke. He's explaining a joke he played on young Lionel.'

This only made things worse. Thoughts tumbled through Mrs McFee's head, but all that came out of her mouth were single words. 'Lionel? . . . Joke? . . . Explain?'

Mrs Boofus laid a comforting hand on her shoulder. With that, and a pause to catch her breath, Mrs McFee regained her composure. 'Explain away,' she said, looking at her husband. 'If anyone here's in need of an explanation, 'tis me.'

The ground began to level out, and growing gaps appeared between the trees. Lionel and Rarty emerged, blinking, from the fringes of the wood, and crossed the clumps of tussocky grass to the beach. The soft sea sounds whispered welcome, and they could taste salt in the fog, which hung in thin wisps round their shoulders, like ghostly cloaks.

Rarty stopped above the beach, whose size meant it could only be Logger's Strand. She had found it. She took pride in her navigation but, remembering it was Lionel's idea to come here, she turned to him for further guidance. 'Right or left?' she asked.

He had no idea. He stared in both directions. The beach hadn't looked nearly so big from the sea. It seemed better to walk westwards towards the fog-shrouded sun, now growing orange as it dropped towards its horizon rendezvous. 'Right,' he said boldly, as if he knew what he was talking about.

To reach the beach they had to cross the bank of

washed-up trees, tangled together like a stack of old bones, worn white and smooth as ivory by the ceaseless sea. Lionel clambered over, dropped down on to the soft pale sand – the scrasser – and turned to help Rarty. She was obviously in pain from her bruises but would not take his hand. *Too proud for your own good*, thought Lionel. He and the dogs watched her struggle down, then set off sunwards alongside her.

'Why wouldn't you let me help you?' Lionel asked. 'Is it because I'm a boy?'

Rarty didn't answer at first, but a small smile crept across her face. 'No,' she said. 'It's because I'm a girl.'

At first the dogs, glad to be on a beach again, ran about at random, chasing each other in circles and splashing through the surf. They soon sensed the serious mood of their young companions and, without any bidding, settled down to walk quietly at heel.

Lionel was amazed to see how the knotted trees formed an almost unbroken wall. They must have lain there a long time, for tall bunches of marram grass grew up between them. Further west, as the beach curved more sharply, the wall became irregular, interrupted by gaps which led to strips of sand, enclosed between the dead trees on the beach and the live ones in the forest. None of these had been visible from the *Colleen* yesterday, and all of them had to be searched.

It took longer than they'd expected to survey the beach, but eventually they neared the end, where the timber petered out, and the sand gave way to jagged rocks. Rarty looked at Lionel. He knew what she was thinking. 'That's only half the beach,' he said, trying to convince himself as much as to persuade her. 'If she's not here, she'll be at the other end.'

Rarty said nothing as they turned round to retrace their steps. She was suddenly aware of an absence. 'The dogs,' she said. 'Where have the dogs gone?'

There was a clamorous burst of barking from the other side of the wooden wall. Lionel and Rarty were puzzled: they had seen no gap. Then they spotted a narrow break, easily missed when walking westwards, but much more obvious now.

Rarty dashed through the gap ahead of Lionel, but both stopped abruptly on the far side. Here at last – stranded, riven by gashes, broken-finned – lay Gumnor with the dogs dancing loudly beside her.

Rarty fell to her knees beside the poor creature's battered head, and Lionel watched, stricken, as she ran her fingers gently over the cruel red-ribbon wounds on Gumnor's flank. The dogs calmed down and backed off to stand beside Lionel, growling softly, hackles raised.

Rarty began to stroke Gumnor's head, and Lionel could see from the shake of her shoulders that she was crying, hard but silently. He wanted to comfort her, but something told him to hold back. This was Rarty's moment, painful though it was to see it, and he had to wait till it was done. He could comfort her later.

Rarty didn't care who saw or heard her. They had found her Gumnor at last, but they were too late. She was dead. Nothing else mattered. 'I'm sorry, Gumnor,' she kept saying over and over. 'I'm sorry. We tried so hard, me and Pa and Ma and Lionel and everybody. We've been everywhere. I'm sorry.' She rested her head against the huge creature, sobbing uncontrollably. 'And now it's too late.'

Lionel watched with a lump in his throat. Rarty's arms were outstretched, running all over the massive head, feeling again the smoothness of her silvery scales. Some of them brushed off and fell unseen at her feet, to glitter on the sand like frozen tears. Lionel took a step forward, but again something about her stopped him. Her sobbing had ceased, and she was perfectly still. Her left hand lay on Gumnor's nose, her fingers over one of the two great blowholes in the creature's snout. Something on her fingers – she couldn't be sure – wait – yes. A coolness, barely noticeable, nothing more.

Then warm. Cool again. Warm. Cool. She was sure now.

She bent her head to wipe her eyes, then whispered over her shoulder. 'She's alive. She's still breathing . . . but only just. Come and see.'

Lionel knelt close beside her, one hand on her right shoulder, and the other outstretched, as hers was, to Gumnor's nose. She intertwined his fingers with her own and held them over the blowhole, looking at him all the while, with a question in her eyes. Could he feel it too?

Lionel didn't meet her gaze at first. He closed his eyes, the better to concentrate, and waited. It was important to be sure. Rarty grew impatient. 'Well?' she asked.

'I'm counting,' he whispered back.

'*Counting*? But –'

'Shhh.' He waved her to silence. 'Eight . . . nine . . . ten . . . and change. One . . . two . . . three . . . four.' He opened his eyes and looked at her. 'It's the same each time. Cool for ten – the inbreath, then warm for four – the outbreath. She *is* alive.'

Rarty smiled at him through her tears. Lionel smiled back. She couldn't be sure – was he crying too? Then they both felt embarrassed about continuing their embrace, and stood up quickly, with an urgent need to do something.

Rarty whipped off her hat and handed it to Lionel.

'Can you collect some water in this?' she asked. He ran off surfwards. Rarty looked round. They had to refloat her. The tide was coming in, but wouldn't reach this high and, anyway, the wooden barricade blocked the way. It would have to go. She tugged frantically at the topmost logs, struggling to loosen them.

Lionel returned with a hatful of water to see a log crash to the sand, narrowly missing Port's tail and Starboard's feet. The dogs retreated to a safe distance, but Rarty continued her frenzied work, oblivious to the danger. She broke off when she saw Lionel, took the cap from him, and returned to Gumnor's side. She carefully trickled water over Gumnor's sand-glued eyes, washing their dead-fish dullness away. There was a glimmer of life about the poor creature now.

Lionel ran back for more water, wondering if Gumnor could still see or if she knew who Rarty was. When he returned Rarty was already back at work on the driftwood. 'Just splash it on her head,' she said. Lionel obeyed. 'And now help me. We've got to get her back into the water somehow.'

Lionel was astonished. 'We'll never be able to move her. She's so big.'

'If we can't bring her to the water, we'll have to bring the water to her,' replied Rarty, her voice brimming with

159

determination. 'Here.' She handed him a narrow log with a flattened end. 'You dig. I'll move the wood.' They set to work.

The dogs stood by, ill at ease, watching; watching Lionel, watching Rarty, but most of all watching Gumnor.

Lionel soon found himself sweating, breathless and covered in sand. He straightened to remove his jumper, and was amazed to see how much wood Rarty had moved already. She was pulling the barricade apart and dragging it aside with a desperate energy, all her injuries forgotten. His own efforts at digging a channel seemed feeble by comparison. Lionel observed her, as he hung his jumper on a log behind him, and felt the doubts begin to grow. Rarty might work furiously – so might he – but the best efforts of two children would never shift enough wood and sand to bring the sea to Gumnor, and even if they did, what then? What if she just floated around? She looked far too weak to do anything else. Was she even conscious?

He dropped his stick and joined Rarty. 'We can't do this on our own,' he said quietly. Rarty paused. Lionel saw the way the wood had torn her hands, and winced. She hadn't even noticed. She looked at Gumnor, then the sea, then the sun, and when she spoke the words came in short bursts.

'An hour, maybe two . . . till high tide . . . dark then too.' She looked at the results of Lionel's digging. 'Perhaps you're right.'

He felt criticised. 'Maybe if I go for help? I can run – you can't.'

'You might get lost.'

'I'll take the dogs. They won't.'

'Just one. Take Port. Starboard can stay.'

Lionel agreed and led Port away in a steady trot. When he looked over his shoulder he could see Starboard staring after them and, behind him, Rarty atop the barricade, flinging logs to the ground as the fog thickened round her.

'We've waited long enough,' said Mrs McFee. 'I think we should go.' Waldo nodded.

Mrs Boofus was unsure. 'What if they get back to find we're gone?'

'We could leave a note,' said Will. 'Tell about Waldo and Lionel and Logger's Strand and such. Or you could stay.'

'I don't know,' said Mrs Boofus, wringing her hands and pacing about. Lon should have been back ages ago. All he had to do was go to Parson's Peak. It could only mean Rarty wasn't there. 'I just don't know.'

'Come with us, Mrs B,' said Jeb. 'I'll write them a note.'

Mrs Boofus relented. 'All right,' she said. 'If you think it's for the best.' She fussed with her coat while Jeb scribbled a message and left it propped against a sextant on Waldo's chart table. They joined Will and Mrs McFee at the door, but all four were halted on the threshold by a loud cough and a trundling sound.

They looked round to see Waldo propelling himself forward in his clumsy wheelchair, amid much puffing and grunting, his teeth gritted with the effort. At the door he stopped, looked each of them in the eye in turn and opened his mouth to speak. Out came a halting, wheezy whisper, but the words he spoke were distinct enough. 'I'm . . . coming . . . too,' he said. This was not a request.

No one knew what to say. He had neither spoken nor been on board any kind of vessel for years, yet here he was demanding, in that no-nonsense way he'd had long before, that they take him along, wheelchair and all.

Will reacted first. He was glad to see Waldo so changed, whatever the reason might be. He'd been without a father for so long. He stepped behind the chair and gripped the handles firmly as the others parted before the door. 'Aye aye, sir,' he said. 'I'll pipe you aboard myself.'

* * *

Port's eager fitness had him trotting on ahead, then stopping for Lionel, over and over. They were deep in the wood, and although at first it had seemed familiar, Lionel now felt uneasy, for he had no idea where they were, and had little choice but to trust himself to a dog.

Port allowed him no rest. He would dash ahead as Lionel approached, leaving the lad toiling behind, too afraid of separation to risk even the briefest of breaks. Lionel grew exhausted, and his progress ever slower, as the hillside steepened. He tried desperately to keep Port – 'Holy Grail Hound' he renamed him – in view but, on an especially steep rise, he had to plod head-down, almost on all fours, and when he next looked up he saw what he most feared: no dog.

Before Lionel could find the breath to whistle or call he heard a distant barking and the crackle of twigs as Port dashed off through the trees. Lancelot didn't have to put up with this, he thought. His chalice never tore off questing after squirrels. Why me?

Lionel shouted as loud as he could, then listened. Silence. He suddenly felt very alone in a fog-bound, darkening wood, and his spirit began to fail him. He tried a whistle. Again nothing. He slumped to the pine-needle ground and groaned. The silence he and Rarty had drunk in on their way to the beach now threatened to drown him. He was lost, just like she'd said he would be. He'd lost the dog. He didn't even know how to find his way back to the beach to help her. He had failed her, his Guinevere, just when she needed him most. He was useless. He leaned against a birch tree and began to rock back and forth, humming tunelessly under his breath, his head in his hands. He felt empty and worthless and wretched and very, very small, a Lancelot no more. He wished he were dead.

As they descended through the wood, John Quarrie and Mr Boofus took parallel paths about fifty yards apart. From time to time a clump of rocks or a fallen tree would force them together for a while, before they parted for their separate searching. On the third of these occasions Mr Boofus noticed John Quarrie's limp had eased. 'Walking better then, John?' he asked.

'Aye, it is and all,' came the reply. John Quarrie patted his belly. 'Though I do feel the want of Flossie's broth, Lon.'

Mr Boofus grinned. 'That I share. My old guts are yowling like I'd swallowed a cat. Scarce hear my own footfalls at times.' A sudden pattering among the trees ahead abruptly ended their chatter, and both men stiffened to see what it was that approached. Port burst upon them, panting and anxious. He jumped up, slavering, to paw at their waists.

Mr Boofus frowned as he patted some calm into the frantic beast. 'Oh my,' he said. 'What does this mean, boy? Where's your brother? And what of the wains, eh?' He looked at John Quarrie, who shrugged.

Mr Boofus kept talking to Port, asking him soft-toned questions in an effort to soothe him, but his worries showed through. 'What's happened, boy?' He crouched down. 'Where are they all? Can you find 'em for us?'

John Quarrie stood back. 'I doubts it, Lon,' he muttered. 'He must a' dashed off after rabbit or some such, an' got sep'rated. He were panicky like that on account of he's lost. They could be anywhere.'

Port was calmer now. Mr Boofus straightened up, wincing at the stiffness in his knees. 'Then I s'pose we'll just have to carry on down the way. Come along now, boy.'

They set off downhill once more, retracing Port's steps as best they could. The dog stuck close by, at least to begin with, starting at every call or whistle. After a mile or so, Mr Boofus noticed a sudden change in him. He stopped, head high to sniff the air, then trotted backwards and forwards, zigzagging between the trees, his nose ploughing a furrow in the fallen leaves.

'He's got a scent, John,' said Mr Boofus.

'Aye, but of what, I wonder?' John Quarrie wasn't convinced. 'Squirrel, maybe? Rabbit? Marten? Or maybe his own from the way up?'

Port set off at a fast walk through the trees to the left, raising his head only to check they were following. 'Come on, John,' said Mr Boofus as he led the pursuit. 'He's on to them.'

John Quarrie followed in silence. He needed all his breath to match the pace that Port was setting. *If that beast don't slow down he'll lose hisself all over, and us besides*, he thought.

Mrs McFee studied her husband in disbelief. He was transformed. He sat in his chair at the stern of the *Colleen* as she puttered parallel to Gallican's shore. His face, so mask-like for so many years, cracked into a wide and vivid smile as he stared upwards at imagined masts. He turned to Will, who stood by his side, and spoke in telegraphic-order tones, familiar from long ago. 'Trim her mizzen and fore, number one.' His voice was still croaky but his fluency was coming back fast. 'Little enough wind, number one. Use it to the full, shall we?'

Will was at first unsure how to respond, but a quick

smile from his mother confirmed his instincts. He saluted smartly. 'Mizzen an' fore. Aye aye, cap'n.'

Jeb in the wheelhouse turned round at the sound of his father's voice. Waldo gimlet-eyed him. 'What heading there, helmsman?'

Jeb checked the compass. 'Two four eight,' he called back.

'Two four eight be blowed,' roared Waldo. 'West south west I asked for, sir, and west south west I shall have, God damn your eyes.'

'Aye aye, cap'n,' said Jeb as he turned back to the wheel with a broad grin on his face. A heading of 248° *was* west south west, of course, but he remembered from years before his father's unaccountable hatred of numerical bearings. He'd never understood it, but he was glad to see it lived again so fiercely.

From her perch on the lobster pots Mrs Boofus watched all this with pale bemusement. She wasn't seasick yet but she was queasily anxious she soon would be. She didn't understand where they were going or why, or what was happening to Waldo. He met her puzzled gaze, then eyed in turn the horizon and the sun's position in the sky above it.

He held her eye and called to Jeb, 'What speed, helmsman?'

'Six knots steady, sir,' Jeb replied. He was enjoying this.

Waldo smiled. 'Fear not, Elna,' he said. 'Gumnor by nightfall, for sure.'

Mrs McFee's composure finally broke. She fell to her knees at his feet. 'Waldo . . . Husband . . .' she sobbed. 'You're back at last. Back here with us. With me.' She buried her face in his lap.

He laid his hand gently on her grey bowed head. Her hair had been red the last time he'd touched it so. 'Aye, love,' he said softly. 'Aye. And a long cold voyage it's been.' He slipped his hand under her chin to raise her head, meeting her tear-filled eyes with his own. 'But back I am to stay.'

A cold wet nose on his brow and a warm wet tongue on his face shook Lionel out of his keening. He opened his eyes to see Port, so close he wasn't in focus, standing before him in look-what-I've-found triumph. Behind the dog grew a forest of legs, the thick-hewn tree-trunk legs of John Quarrie and Lon Boofus, stolid and still. Lionel didn't dare look up, so fearful was he of their anger, dropping like apples from above.

In place of an apple, an acorn. 'All right there, lad?' asked John Quarrie in a gruff but concerned tone. Lionel still couldn't look up or speak, but he did manage a nod.

Mr Boofus's irritation broke through. 'Then what's all this head-in-hands humming for?' he demanded.

Lionel's relief at being found faded to dismay at the way they had found him. He swallowed hard. He would have to bluff. 'A dog-return chant of the ancients,' he said, affecting a nonchalant calm as he got to his feet. 'I wasn't sure it would work.' He bent to brush the leaves from his legs. 'I kept trying it till I remembered it right.' He straightened and indicated the two grown-ups. 'And here we are, awash with witnesses that it did.'

John Quarrie looked at Mr Boofus, tapping his temple and shaking his head. Mr Boofus's irritation flowered into outright anger. 'Now, lad, enough of your nonsense,' he blustered. 'What about –'

Lionel calmly cut him short. 'We've found her, Mr Boofus. Me and Rarty. Rarty and me. We've found your Gumnor.'

There was a silence. Mr Boofus couldn't take it in. Lionel watched him struggle to comprehend, then went on, anticipating the questions that didn't come. 'Beached, on Logger's Strand. Alive, yes, but . . . We've got to be quick.'

Rarty was exhausted. When she wiped her forearm

across her brow, her sweat mingled with the bloodied seawater on her wood-cut hands. She had moved enough logs to clear Gumnor's way to the sea; but digging the channel was painfully slow. Her improvised spade was better than nothing, but not by much, and the wet sand fell back into the hole almost as fast as she could dig it out. Lionel had been right – they did need help. But where was he? Why was he taking so long?

She looked at her tattered hands. Now, as she tired, she felt the salt sting in their wounds, and flinched as she splashed wake-up water on her face, and then over Gumnor, who still stared seawards with sightless eyes. Rarty returned to her labours with a sigh, flinging the sand high behind her as she dug.

Along the beach, Lionel pointed out this sandstorm. 'There,' he said, 'that's where she is.' Port saw it too and ran on ahead, a blur of flying legs.

John Quarrie watched him go. 'Maybe we should be eatin' dog food, Lon,' he said. Lionel looked at him, an unvoiced appeal in his eyes. John Quarrie knew what he wanted. 'Aye, lad. On you go, as well,' he said, and Lionel trotted off in Port's footsteps.

Port greeted his brother with a loud display of barking and raised forepaws. Rarty looked up as Lionel arrived. 'Dr Livingstone, I presume,' he called.

She dropped her spade with a smile. 'What kept you?' she asked.

'A little trouble with squirrels,' said Lionel. He waved at the two old sailors approaching behind him. 'But I found them in the end.'

'You didn't get lost then?' asked Rarty sceptically.

'Lost? Oh no, of course not,' he said airily.

Mr Boofus stood by Rarty's channel, aghast at the sight before him, and ignored Lionel's denials.

'She's very weak, Pa,' Rarty said, following her father as he walked slowly round the poor beast, his hands tracing the wounds on her flank and the awkward angle of her broken fin. 'I thought we were too late when we first found her.'

Mr Boofus cast an eye over the scattered logs and Rarty's shredded fingers. 'You've done grand, lass,' he said. Rarty could tell he was upset, but knew he wouldn't show it. He stroked her cheek tenderly. 'Done grand indeed. And while there's life in her there's hope yet. You've given her every chance you could. Let's finish the job, shall we?' He rummaged among the logs for some more makeshift spades, handing out one each to John Quarrie and Lionel, and keeping the biggest for himself. Seeing this, Rarty picked hers up once more and returned to her stretch of the channel.

The four of them spread out between Gumnor and the encroaching surf and began to dig, ferociously at first, then more steadily as they each withdrew into their private digging worlds.

Lionel listened to the grunts beside him and the erratic scrunch of shovels in the sand. Something was missing. Listening now to the steady crash of waves breaking on the shore, like the ocean's breath, he had it. 'We should sing, to set a rhythm,' he shouted. 'Altogether. It'll be easier that way.'

John Quarrie dug away, excavating memory along with sand, and sang out in a rough but musical voice:

> Anchors aweigh, lads, anchors aweigh,
> The lasses bid us tarry, but we know we may not stay,
> For the tide it is a-turning, and the sea she sings her call,
> And if we are to answer, 'tis now or not at all.

After a line or two Mr Boofus recognised the song and listened to the rest with a lump in his throat. When the singing stopped, he swallowed hard, called out, 'Again, John,' and this time sang along.

Lionel and Rarty dug on, already in the rhythm,

listening to the words and the way they fell. The third time round they joined in too. Locked together by the cadence of the sea-shanty, the four of them strove on, singing over and over till they were hoarse. The sand seemed to fly away and the channel deepened and widened with each verse.

Rarty, digging close beside Gumnor, felt hope rise anew within her. The fog was thickening, dusk was drawing close, and the tide was about to turn, but it began to look as if they might just do it. Soon they could break through the last few feet to the sea, bringing the water of life bubbling up to Gumnor, and then – hope beyond hope – bearing Gumnor back to her home.

Mr Boofus, who was working closest to the water, watched each wave, marking in his mind the limit of its reach. It wouldn't be long now. He straightened up, one hand rubbing his back. 'What d'you say, John? Break her through now or dig some more?' Rarty listened intently.

John Quarrie stopped digging and joined him at the water's edge. 'I'd say now, Lon. She may need time to come round, and we can still dig with water in the trench, if need be.' They redoubled their efforts for the last few feet.

'Here it comes!' yelled Lionel, tossing his stick aside, and stepping back to admire his efforts as the foaming water swept past his feet. It reached Rarty in a trickle and then a swelling flood, and began to lap around Gumnor's head.

John Quarrie and Mr Boofus continued to work on the trench, though the water-weighted sand was sloppy now, while Lionel joined Rarty by Gumnor's side, splashing the chilly salt water all over her.

'Come on, Gumnor,' said Rarty. 'Wake up. You've got to wake up now.' There was no response.

Lionel checked her breathing. 'Ten and four still, just like before' he said. He thought it was fainter, too, but he didn't tell her that.

Rarty glanced over to her father and John Quarrie. The fog and the twilight were thickening by the minute, and their outlines were already woolling over, but she could see well enough to know that they had stopped work, and were walking towards her in a heavy-legged gait that spelt defeat.

'I fear 'tis no use, lass,' said Mr Boofus flatly. 'Tide's turned.'

Rarty grew desperate. 'Wake *up*, Gumnor. Wake up, please.' Her father watched her splashing knee-deep in the sandy brine, until he could watch no more, and stepped in to join her. He gently prised the spade from her blood-sticky grasp, and placed an arm round her shoulders. 'Time to stop, love. There's times to plug on, and to watch you fightin' so makes your old pa right proud, but there's also times to stand back and to know you can do no more.' He could feel her sobbing. Her shoulders shuddered and she hung her head. 'This is one such. We've done all we could, lass. All anybody could.' She didn't want to agree, but he took her silence and the end to her splashing as assent.

The four of them stood close beside Gunnor, feeling their sweat chill as the foggy twilight deepened. John Quarrie patted Lionel's head. 'You can sail with me anytime, lad,' he said, and Lionel knew that what had happened in the woods was forgotten in the shared sadness of this moment.

The silence seemed to grow with each breaking wave as they huddled together beside their huge dying creature. Just then, when there seemed nothing to sense but sorrow, they were all startled by a sound out to sea, a sound at once so familiar but so unexpected and so out of place. A foghorn was calling close by, where no ship would ever come. All but Rarty looked to their left, puzzled and straining, but there was nothing; no lights but the flashing of surf, no movement but the heave of waves. Then the sound came again, doubled, quadrupled, gathering volume and depth till it filled the air.

Not far offshore, but unseen from the beach, Jeb swung the humming-hulled *Colleen* round. He looked at Waldo and the women, who sat transfixed by the sound, and then at his brother. 'I know,' said Will. 'Twice in one day, eh?'

Rarty's eyes had never left Gumnor. 'Pa!' she shouted. 'Pa, look! She's moving!' And so she was. It was barely perceptible at first – a deepening of breath, a quiver of fin, a tremor in her tail. But as the foghorn chorus rose around them, her movements quickened and gathered purpose and then, slowly but surely, Gumnor began to wriggle her awkward way to the sea.

'We have to help her,' yelled Rarty, and set to again with her spade. Lionel followed suit. John Quarrie looked at Mr Boofus, who spread his hands and shrugged. Neither understood, but both took up their spades once more and joined Rarty in heaving and digging and splashing Gumnor to the shore.

Halfway there she fell still again, and all progress stopped. They could only help her if she moved herself, and now she seemed exhausted. Mr Boofus approached to check her breathing, afraid he'd find only a final stillness. He placed his hand over one blowhole and paused. His relief at the cooling inflow over his fingers was visible but shortlived, for no warming outflow followed. She was breathing, yes, but breathing in and in and in and . . .

He was knocked on his back by a huge foghorn call, emanating from deep within Gumnor and thundering out to the world. I'm here, it seemed to say. I'm still alive.

In the pause that followed, the offshore foghorns dimmed then responded with vigour anew, willing Gumnor to drag herself across the last few yards that separated her from the sea and salvation, welcoming her back to freedom and an end to her loneliness.

As Gumnor neared the water, Rarty stopped digging in front of her, and grinned at her pa, who understood without words. Gumnor needed their help no more. She was going to make it.

Seeing this though, Rarty felt a terrible pull. If – when – Gumnor did reach the sea, she would be gone again. The only way to save her was to let her go. Mr Doofus saw it too but, like Rarty, he knew there was no choice. He bent to shout in her ear over the foghorn orchestra. 'It's better this way,' he said. Rarty smiled back at him through a face streaked with tears. He was right. They had found Gumnor, they had helped save her, they had watched her return to her own when they thought she had none. But it still hurt more than any broken bone to know they'd never see her again.

Before them, Gumnor slipped into the deepening water and the waves crashed over her head. She lay there a while, her flapping tail still visible at times, and then she was gone.

Rarty found one of her hands gripped by her father, and the other, more tentatively, by Lionel. John Quarrie stood behind her, a hand on each shoulder. Dogs nudged her knees. They listened and watched. The foghorn echoes faded as the hugumnodin herd drew away, past the *Colleen*, to sea. Then, just as they thought the spectacle was over, the water cleft violently before them, as a massive head, twice the size of Gumnor's and covered in barnacles, surged up out of the surf and forwards to the shore, with unimagined speed and power. Lionel and the dogs shrank back, but Rarty had no fear, for she could see Gumnor beside him.

There was a rush of air, then the beach beneath them shook and the water boiled, as this enormous apparition thundered its farewell and its thanks. The blast went on and on, then ceased as abruptly as it had begun, and the silence that followed was total. Even the sea seemed still. All the other foghorns had stopped. Gumnor, her companion, the herd, all were gone. It was over.

Rarty watched on for a time, then turned to her father. 'She's lost for ever now, isn't she, Pa?'

'No, love. I'd say she's just been found.'

CHAPTER TEN
SLÂN GARAITH

YELLOW LIGHT SPILLED LIKE HONEY FROM THE
ferry's portholes on to the oil-black harbour water, as
the vessel drew up to Gallican's quay. Rarty shivered,
deep inside her December coat, and scanned the ship's
railings above. He wasn't there. Just like him to miss the
boat, she thought.

Then came a loud shout from the stern. 'Mrs Noah!'
he called out, waving an outstretched arm. 'Mrs Noah!
Is your husband in?' His arm dropped to indicate the ferry
beneath him. 'Maybe he'd like this one.'

Rarty laughed and waved back at him. He hadn't
changed. 'Hello, Lionel,' she replied. Several of the quayside
crowd were stifling giggles, but one Sunday-school type
flicked her grey-eyed glare back and forth between Lionel
and Rarty, ship and shore, tutting primly all the while.

The ferrymen tied up and lowered the gangwalk. Four or five well-wrapped figures waddled down it, bearing the harvest of their cityside market trip. Lionel was the last. Buried in an old duffle coat two sizes too big, he struggled ashore under the weight of two large bags, which fell to the ground with a thump as he returned Rarty's warm hug of welcome.

'I didn't think it would be so dark,' he said. 'It's only four.'

'Shortest day today,' said Rarty. Darkness had been hastened by the heavy clouds which had growled about the horizon since noon, then smothered the sickly sun before it reached its bed. 'Probably the coldest too.' She pulled up the hood of his coat. 'Let's get inside quick, shall we, before those pixie ears of yours freeze and fall off.'

She bent to pick up one of his bags and gasped at the unexpected weight. 'You're only staying a week, Lionel.' She put the bag down again. 'What on earth have you got in here?'

'Books,' he replied. He handed her the lighter bag and swung the other on to his back with a grunt. 'You said to bring some, remember?'

'*Some*, yes, but not a whole library.' She shouldered the bag he offered her, and they set off along the quay. 'You'll never read all these.'

'Already have. I got out all my favourites and couldn't decide which not to bring.' He was already puffing under his load. 'I can leave most of them here – they won't be missed.'

'How did you get them down to the ferry?' She wondered if his family had seen him off. 'Did anyone help?'

He shook his head and looked away briefly, then met her eye again and smiled. 'Wheelbarrow,' he said.

She tried to picture it – a duffel-coated barrow boy trundling bags of books through darkening city streets to the wharf. He was probably whistling. Giggling to herself at the image, she led him up the cobbled street.

Passing the McFees' cottage Lionel slowed, as if to stop, but Rarty walked on. 'We'll not bother them just now,' she said. 'They're coming over tomorrow. You can see them then.'

A little further on Lionel stopped to rest his aching shoulders. The lane was so dark he could hardly see his feet. Far below the lights of Gallican's harbour sparkled brightly, and not-yet-shuttered cottage windows glowed their warm farewells to the ferry, which was already leaving for Jetta and the mainland, an oasis of lights in a desert of blackness. 'Do you like it here?' he asked.

She didn't hesitate. 'Yes. More and more. I think I'm

an islander, really,' she said brightly. 'Ma's got the cottage looking really nice, and I like my new room. Pa put hammock bars in.' She watched the ferry go. Soon it would pass by her old home, all empty now, and then under the bridge, near the square grey box that housed the new foghorn. She resumed in a softer, sadder voice. 'I miss the old place,' she said, with a sigh. 'But it's not the same with Gumnor gone.'

'What'll happen to it?' asked Lionel.

'Don't know. The harbour people want to sell it. Some people came to look just before we left. Rich citysiders, you know, after a holiday home.' She remembered with scorn the way one of their children had turned up her nose at Rarty's room. 'I can't *possibly* sleep here, Mama,' she had whined. 'It's *so* poky.'

'I don't think they'll want it though,' said Rarty. 'Stairs too steep for their precious daughter, if you catch my meaning.'

Lionel pretended to be horrified. 'You didn't.'

'I did. She didn't fall far. Screeched fit to burst, but it was only bruises.' A mischievous grin lit up her face. 'No one else came round till we left.'

She fumbled in her pockets for a torch to light their way. 'Come on,' she said, hoisting her bag again. 'It's not far.'

They walked on up the hill, Rarty shining the torch to their left, looking for the gate. The beam flickered across something pale. Lionel stopped for a closer look while Rarty illuminated it for him. A piece of weathered planking, rubbed smooth by the sea and then smoother still by human hand, was set in the hedge. It bore some lettering, burnt into the frost-sparkled surface: *Slân Garaith*.

Lionel frowned. 'Who's Sam Garret?' he asked.

She cuffed him playfully round the ear. 'It's islander,' she said. 'You say it differently from the way it looks. Like this: shlarn garaythe.'

Lionel tried it out several times. 'I like the sound,' he said. 'It's like the sea. What does it mean?'

'Coming home.' She opened the gate. 'Not the kind of coming home you do at the end of the day. More like after a long voyage away.'

'Your pa did it then?' Lionel asked, though it occurred to him that slân garaith applied to Waldo, and even to Gumnor, as much as to her father. She nodded. Perhaps he'd meant it that way.

Rarty pushed through the gate ahead of him and stopped to hold it open. A pair of bright eyes reflected back greenly the torch's glare as Captain Peg crossed the crunchy lawn to greet them. Lionel bent to stroke him, but recoiled abruptly, his nose curled up, when a small furry bundle, still warm and twitching, dropped into his hand.

Rarty laughed. 'Not another one, surely, Peg.' She dangled the mouse in front of the light to check it was dead. 'There's so many of them, inside and out, with the house being empty so long. And now, with the cold, they're all coming in from the fields. Peg can't catch them fast enough.' She whirled the dead rodent round by its tail and slung it far into the darkness.

Lionel shuddered. There were probably owls about too. 'Let's get inside,' he said.

Rarty opened the front door and ushered him into a house transformed from the dusty shell he'd last seen two months before. He set down his bag and stood there, blinking in the bright light of the hall, and taking in the clean sharp smells of fresh paint and heather. Mrs Boofus stepped in from the kitchen and held out her arms. 'Hello, love,' she beamed, smothering him in a motherly embrace. 'Lovely to see you again.' She released him and indicated the hall. 'What do you think?'

'You've been busy,' he said. He was reminded of an abandoned vessel, lovingly restored. 'It's very . . . shipshape. I'd hardly have known it.'

Mrs Boofus guided them towards the stairs. 'We'll be

quiet just now, Rarty. Your pa's dozing by the fire. Why don't you show Lionel up to your room, to drop his things, then pop back down for some tea.'

Lionel and Rarty struggled upstairs with his heavy bags to her corner room. Two hammocks, plump-pillowed, dangling blankets and all, swung from the beams, perpendicular to each other like the arms of an L. 'No bed at all?' he asked.

Rarty shook her head. 'Hammocks and nothing but. I wouldn't have it any other way.'

Lionel unbuttoned his coat and reached into an inside pocket. He pulled out a small package, carefully wrapped in green crêpe paper. 'I brought you something,' he said, as he handed it to her. 'More like giving it back, really.'

Rarty was intrigued. Lionel watched, feeling awkward, as she unwrapped his gift, peeling aside the layers to reveal a smooth translucent amber block. She looked puzzled for a moment, then held it to the light and gasped at the beauty of the copper-coloured leaf within, reflecting gold and red and orange glints through the perfect clarity of amber. She stared at it a long time, then turned to him.

'The wood, here on Gallican, the day we found Gumnor,' she said. She remembered how she had lowered this same leaf on to his patient palm. It seemed so long ago.

He smiled agreement. 'Yes,' he said. 'I found it in my shirt pocket.'

She tapped the amber. 'But how did you –?'

'Craft class,' he interrupted.

'So that's where you snuck off to every Tuesday,' she laughed, clutching the present to her chest, then holding it at arm's length to admire it once more. 'It's lovely, Lionel. Thank you so much.' She hugged him. He didn't know what to do. Eventually his embarrassed stiffness was broken, to his relief, by a call from Mrs Boofus below.

'Tea's ready, youngsters.'

They trooped down, suddenly hungry, and burst into the front room in a flurry of chatter. Mr Boofus sat by the fire, no longer asleep, but working away at something. He was startled by the sudden intrusion, and put a bulky, half-glimpsed object to one side, where it was hidden by his chair. He then stood up briskly to greet them.

'What ho, lad,' he boomed. 'Welcome aboard.' Lionel felt a powerful arm descend on his shoulder like a yoke. 'Come away into the galley.' He was propelled into the kitchen, and pressed down into a chair at one end of a heavily laden table. Some wood shavings spiralled down from Mr Boofus's sausagey fingers, to catch in the wool of Lionel's jumper. He pretended not to notice. They were hiding something from him.

'We're just going outside. We may be gone some time,' said Lionel, as he laced up his imaginary snowshoes. Rarty opened the door to a garden all crystal-hush white, its crisp stillness a-shimmer under the low sun. They had watched the snowfall begin from their hammocks the night before, and it had continued its stealthy muffling throughout the hours of darkness. Lionel and Rarty could scarcely contain themselves over the briefest of breakfasts, and now, at last, they were free to venture outside.

Lionel, who had been locked into his Scott of the Antarctic role since the moment of waking, raised his head, squinting, as he stepped outside. 'Blizzard's done,' he said, turning to Rarty, his Captain Oates. 'I say we shake out the huskies and make a bid for the Pole. Are you game?'

She played along. 'Ready for anything. Let's away to base camp and dog up at once, shall we?' They set off downhill through ankle-deep snow, astonished at the way their underfoot scrunching rang loud through the bird-stilled silence all about.

Down at base camp, Mrs McFee greeted them warmly, explained that Waldo wasn't up yet, though her sons were long gone. She gladly handed over a couple of dogs even more excited by the snowfall than the explorers who'd come to collect them.

'Mush,' yelled Lionel, as Rarty handed him the leashes. The dogs bounded forward, with unexpected power. Lionel took a few staggering steps then fell full-length in the snow, to be dragged face-down for yards before he managed to let go. He rolled over to lie on his back, spitting out snow between bursts of laughter.

Once her own laughter was stilled, Rarty called back the dogs, who returned at length to lick at Lionel as he sat up, beating the snow out of his hair. 'Stronger than you think, you boys,' he said. 'Must be all that penguin meat.'

'What *are* you doing, Lionel?' asked Rarty. He was kneeling by a birch trunk, peering downhill at the dark shapes of Port and Starboard as they flitted between the trees below.

'Watching for wolves,' he whispered.

'But there aren't any wolves in Antarctica.'

'I know. There aren't any trees either. And since

there's trees all around' – he patted the mossy trunk – 'we must be somewhere else. Canada. Trapper Joe and his Huron squaw, sledding east with a load of beaver pelts. Wolves closing in, no bullets left, night drawing nigh –'

A snowball exploded on the side of his head. 'Huron squaw?' yelled Rarty, hurling another hard-packed missile, which he managed to dodge. 'Huron squaw?' She bent to gather more ammunition. 'I'll give you Huron squaw, No Bullets Joe.'

Lionel thought about fighting but decided it was safer to surrender. He stood up, hands held high. 'All right, all right,' he said. 'Guilty as charged. I'll come quietly. Sorry.' Another, larger snowball whistled through the trees and hit him square in the chest. 'Hey,' he protested. 'I'm under arrest. Mounties don't –'

He broke off when he saw that her third snowball was still in her hands, and she was looking behind her, mystified. She turned back to him, shrugged, said, 'That wasn't me,' and was herself hit hard in the back, the snow spraying round her in a cloud of fluffy shrapnel. Whoever threw this was strong. They both dropped to their knees and hid behind a tree, looking around for any sign of their invisible attacker.

'The Abominable Snowballman?' ventured Lionel.

'I told you that was a footprint we saw. Bears don't throw snow.'

'Shhh,' said Rarty. 'Why don't the dogs . . .' She felt the first chill of fear.

'What do we do?' asked Lionel, automatically looking to her for guidance.

'We move. You left, me right. Meet at that double-trunk tree. I think that's where they came from.'

Once again he was impressed by her quick thinking and cool command. 'OK,' he said, and set off as directed, dashing from tree to tree in a low skittery zigzag.

Rarty watched him go, trying not to laugh at his stilted gait. She checked for any oncoming snowballs, looked round once more for the dogs, and moved stealthily away.

At the end of their respective arcs, she and Lionel met again. There was no one about, but the snow round the double-trunk tree was heavily trampled, and there were large bootprints everywhere.

'There's loads of them!' said Lionel, alarmed. 'We're doomed.'

'Or just one, stomping about a lot,' replied Rarty, ever sensible.

'That's right, lass,' said a deep voice behind them. Lionel and Rarty swung round, and all their anxiety evaporated when they saw John Quarrie, a dog at each heel, tossing a snowball from one hand to the other. 'As sharp as ever, I see.'

'Mr Quarrie!' Rarty sprang forward to greet him. He tousled her hair with a smile and turned to Lionel. 'And how's young Igor, eh? Or Captain Scott, or Trapper Joe, or whoever it is you are just now?' Lionel grinned silently. For once he could think of nothing to say.

John Quarrie dropped his snowball. 'I'm sent to fetch you two an' these 'ere dogs for lunch. It's way past noon.' He strode briskly uphill, making it clear they were to join him.

'Ma didn't say you were coming,' said Rarty.

'That's on account of she don't know. A surprise, it is. I'll be over with the McFees for supper tonight. Can you keep it secret?' Rarty nodded. 'I've something to show you two later, but you'll only see it if'n you keep mum.'

Lionel loved this: surprises, secrets, mystery. It was going to be a good evening.

A great gale of laughter blew round the table, and Waldo resumed his tale once it ebbed away. 'And then,' he said, 'do you know what the bo'sun said?'

Mr Boofus and John Quarrie knew well enough, for they had heard this story a good many times – indeed, they had been present at the time of its origin – but they delighted in hearing Waldo tell it again after so long, and tell it in the presence of his sons. His voice still had a raspy edge, but it was unmistakably the Waldo they and his wife beside him knew of old. They let him answer his own question.

'The bo'sun said, "You better 'ad, or I'll have my parrot peck out your other eye, you scurvy knave."' The laughter erupted again. This time, when it died, no one spoke, and the shifting of logs in the blazing hearth magnified the silence.

Lionel saw his chance. His curiosity and his reticence had done battle all evening, and he saw it was now or never. 'Mr Quarrie?' he said tentatively. Rarty looked at him and guessed what he wanted. 'Mr Quarrie?' he ventured again, a little louder. John Quarrie was shaken out of his reminiscences of shipboard life.

'Yes, lad?' he asked. Lionel didn't reply.

John Quarrie frowned and stared a while in puzzlement, before sudden recognition struck. 'Aye, lad, aye, of course, of course. You kept your end o' bargain' – they both recalled the expression on Mr Boofus's face when John Quarrie had entered the kitchen along with Waldo, Flossie, Will and Jeb – 'and now I'll keep mine.'

He reached inside his jacket for a crumpled letter.

'You 'member that bumptious naval officer with his snap-to marines orderin' us all about wi' guns an' such?' Lionel and Rarty nodded. 'This 'ere's a note from their commander.' He unfolded it slowly and with a sense of ceremony, then cleared his throat, and began to read:

'Dear Mr Quarrie,
I write in connection with the recent visit paid to your property by officers and men under my command. I was most concerned to hear of the manner in which this visit was made, and apologise unreservedly for any inconvenience accorded you or your young companions. I have spoken to the officer concerned and can assure you there will be no repetition of this unfortunate incident.

It is now public knowledge that our detection systems had sensed much offshore activity of an uncertain nature near this base some days before the incident in question. Indeed, we have reason to believe that one large vessel lay close offshore while another beached, for a time, within our perimeter.

Given the nature of our enterprise here, such activity aroused considerable concern on our part, and I am sure, as a former Navy man, you will *understand our desire to be as thorough as possible in investigating it. It seems the shore party which came to your house may have been somewhat overdiligent in carrying out my orders, but please be assured that any distress they occasioned arose from an excess of zeal, rather than malice, on their part.*

Please accept my good wishes and extend, if you will, my felicitations to Miss Boofus and Master Merry.

Yours sincerely,
Admiral T. F. Huffington-Smythe, RN KCVO

'Nice of 'im, eh?' said John Quarrie.

Lionel asked to look at the letter. 'Felicitations?' he muttered, as he admired the embossed letterhead. 'No one's extended me felicitations in the whole of my life, never mind a double-barrelled admiral.'

Rarty was more concerned with the content of the letter than its style. 'That "vessel" that beached – could that have been Gumnor, do you reckon?' she asked.

'Who knows, love,' replied her father. 'Though t'would be odd to beach once there, then again here on Gallican not long after. It don't make sense.'

'Mmmm,' mumbled Rarty. 'Unless she *meant* to beach there.'

'But why so?'

'Maybe she wanted to get something,' she said. Or leave something behind, she thought to herself, dimly aware of a half-formed idea itching away at the back of her mind. She lapsed into silence, to try and scratch this hazy notion to the surface.

'We'll never know, love, will we?' said her father. He had little use for speculation such as this. Gumnor was gone. They had all watched her go, whether from the beach where they'd worked so hard to save her, or from the *Colleen* as she and her herd passed by on their way out to sea. What use was it to ponder so?

'But, since you speak of Gumnor . . . We've got something for you, lad.' He disappeared into the front room and returned, moments later, bearing whatever it was he had failed to hide from Lionel the day before: a wooden Gumnor, carved in loving detail from a driftwood tree-stump. 'Me an' Waldo made it,' he said, as he set it down on the table for all to admire. There was such a sense of life about the sculpture's flowing lines and its facial expression, that Lionel would not have been at all surprised to see it move.

'It's for all what you did to find Gumnor. You and your clundiff scrasser, and Rarty here. We owe you our thanks,' said Mr Boofus simply, patting Lionel on the shoulder. Everybody smiled and clapped, Waldo the broadest and longest.

'It's also to say thanks for waking me up, lad,' he said. 'I thought about carving an owl, but I'd guess you might run away.' Rarty giggled. 'Come and visit us any time you like. I'll teach you all the islander I know.'

Lionel was overwhelmed. He knew they were all waiting for him to say something, but he didn't think the words would come and he'd probably go all croaky anyway. He cast his eyes round and lit on a large conch shell on the mantelpiece to his left. He stood up and reached out for it, then clambered on to his chair, held the shell up like a trumpet, and let out the loudest, longest foghorn blast he could muster. When all his breath had gone he sat down again, red-faced and wobbly, and everybody clapped once more.

Even the dogs in the hall joined in. But, as the applause within the room died, the barking without grew in intensity and was soon accompanied by the scraping of claws upon wood, out in the hall.

Rarty got up to investigate, accompanied by Mrs Boofus and Will, as the others all watched. The dogs were barking excitedly at the hall cupboard. 'What's all this then, you two?' admonished Will, as he pulled Port and Starboard aside to shush them.

Mrs Boofus frowned. 'Nowt in there but nick-nacks,' she said.

'That and Ma Tooley's ghost,' joked Jeb. No one laughed. Mrs McFee stilled him with a look.

Now that the dogs were quiet they could all hear what had roused them: a strange tapping noise, like a clock, but not so regular and not metallic. Mrs Boofus opened the cupboard, and the tapping grew louder. 'Is there a light?' she asked. Jeb held out a lantern, which Rarty took with her as she stepped inside, crouching low, and trying to pick out the source of the sound among the piled-up things within.

'A squirrel, perhaps, trapped in the wall?' asked Mrs Boofus of her husband, who, along with everyone bar Waldo, was now crowded into the hall to watch. He merely shrugged in reply.

The cupboard went a long way back, getting lower where it formed the base to the staircase. Rarty rummaged around a while, then suddenly knew exactly where to look. She'd spotted the top of her old rucksack, the one she'd taken to the dell with Lionel the day she fell. She hadn't used it since. Moving some old boxes aside, she pulled it out, sneezing in the dusty air, and emerged into the hall once more.

She put the rucksack on the kitchen table and opened

it up without a word. She wanted to be sure before she said anything. Inside was the strange rock she'd found when she fell down the crevice. She'd never looked at it again. The rucksack had simply been tucked away, forgotten, first in one cottage and then in another.

She lifted the rock out, remembering again its lightness and warm mossy surface. There was no doubt now. It was this that was tapping, faster and louder than before.

Rarty began to try to explain while the others all crowded close, but she and they were silenced when a crack appeared in the rock and the tapping thing inside began to break out. The crack enlarged, some fragments broke away and then, abruptly, the rock split apart to reveal, exhausted by its efforts and blinking in the bright light, a miniature Gumnor, identical in every respect to the wooden one beside it, except for the egg-tooth on its snout. There was a collective gasp from round the table.

''Pon my word,' said Mrs Boofus, and she rushed off to fill the bathtub with water.

Rarty looked up, a broad grin splitting her face. 'Gumnor *did* come ashore that day. I knew it. She came ashore to find somewhere safe for this . . . this little creature to hatch.'

Rarty gently lifted the tiny hugumnodin and lowered it gingerly into the bathtub, which Will and Jeb dragged forward. Mrs Boofus continued filling the tub, running the water over the beast's head. At first it lay still, wriggling feebly, but with the third and fourth jugs of water it found some vigour, and began splashing. The logs in the fire hissed and darkened where the water hit them. On the fifth jug the splashing stopped, and the creature let out a cry. Thin, high-pitched and warbly it may have been, but it was recognisable nonetheless as a foghorn, an answer to Lionel's conch-shell call. He tried again, this time without the shell, and was met with an immediate reply. Everyone laughed.

Rarty looked at her father. 'No chains, Pa. Not this one,' she pleaded.

He smiled, shrugging. 'I'm retired, lass. You're foghorn keeper now. Tend 'un as and where you wish.'

There was more splashing. 'You'll need a name,' said Lionel, with a grin. 'I've got some ideas.'